SILENCE

SILENCE

A FACES OF EVIL NOVELLA

DEBRA WEBB

PINK
HOUSE
PRESS

Copyright © 2013 Debra Webb, Pink House Press

PINK HOUSE PRESS
WebbWorks
Huntsville, Alabama

First Edition November 2013

ISBN 10: 0615902251
ISBN 13: 9780615902258

Absolute silence…is the image of death.
~Jean-Jacques Rousseau

CHAPTER ONE

Ten years before OBSESSION, the holiday magic of Christmas touched the lives of Special Agent Jess Harris and Dan Burnett, her first love… a love that would linger for more than two decades before destiny would bring them together once more. But first, Agent Harris must survive the faces of evil.

CHRISTMAS EVE
BIRMINGHAM, ALABAMA, 6:20 P.M.

She should have taken I-459 before she hit Birmingham proper. Traffic was bumper to bumper. Why the hell weren't these people at home already? It was Christmas Eve for heaven's sake!

I think you need that vacation now.

Jess Harris banished Supervisory Special Agent Ralph Gant's voice from her head. Taking a deep breath, she slowed for the exit to Hoover. Lily was going to be more than a little unhappy that Jess was running late. She had promised to be there before seven.

"Not going to happen," she muttered ruefully.

The cell phone in the cup holder chimed as if she'd telegraphed that thought directly to her sister. It wasn't necessary to check the caller ID, it would be Lily. From the moment her sister delivered her first child, she became the matriarch of their relationship as if the rite of passage into motherhood anointed her with a special wisdom Jess didn't possess.

No, that was wrong, the transition happened way before that. Lil had evolved into a pint-sized mom the day their parents hadn't come home. A car crash had stolen them away. Even now the memories of that afternoon made breathing difficult.

She and Lil had been doing homework at the kitchen table when the police arrived to take them away from the only real home they would know until they were adults with places of their own. Despite being just twelve Lil had, on some level, immediately assumed the role abruptly vacated by their mother.

A smile tugged at Jess's lips. Or, maybe Lily Harris Colburn just liked being bossy. After all, she was two years older than Jess.

Summoning a chipper tone, Jess flipped open her cell before the third chime. "Hey, Lil. Almost there."

That was a major stretch of the truth considering she still had to stop and pick up the dessert she'd promised to bring for tomorrow's Christmas dinner. To the best of her memory there was a Publix in Hoover. At least she hoped the store hadn't closed or moved. If it had, she'd just have to wing it. From

Hoover it was maybe another twenty minutes to Lil's house if traffic didn't get even more congested.

Wishful thinking. She glanced at the line of cars waiting to merge.

Jess listened through her sister's patient reminder for her to drive safely and not to forget that the new minister's older son—who just happened to be about Jess's age and single now that his divorce was final—was having dinner with the family tonight.

How could Jess forget?

"I can't wait to meet him." What was one more little deviation from the truth? "I'm making a quick stop at Publix. See you soon." She closed her phone before Lil could protest, tossed it on the passenger seat and let out a big groan. "Why in the world did you do this, Jessie Lee?"

Because you had a moment of weakness after looking death in the face. Because even her new boss had insisted.

As an agent in the field she had danced with death a few times. It went with the territory. The tension she wanted so badly to deny tightened in her chest. But this time the house call she'd made had been different, had hit a little closer to home. Images from those frantic hours before daylight this morning crowded in on her. Scrubbing the backseat of her car and the carpet in the floorboard. No matter how hard she cleaned the smell of desperation and death lingered—at least in her mind.

She banished the chill that tried to invade her bones. Her colleagues at the Bureau would be shocked. Special Agent Jess Harris hadn't taken more than a day here or there in eight years. She wasn't married. Didn't have kids. Never got sick. What did she need with a vacation? That was her motto and she'd stuck to it her entire career.

Stress is cumulative, Agent Harris. There comes a time in every agent's career when they need a break... or they break. That profound statement had summarized her last psychological evaluation. When she'd moved to the Behavioral Analysis Unit two months ago, Gant had mentioned he preferred his profilers take their downtime a little more seriously. She'd smiled and agreed, then promptly dismissed the concept... until around midnight last night. A few hours after that she hastily packed a bag and headed to Alabama.

The reality of just how long it had been since she'd come home had hit Jess squarely between the eyes. Her sister was the only family she had left in this world—at least the only family she claimed anyway. Jess was not allowing another holiday to pass without spending it with her family even if that decision meant coming *here*.

Coming back here was... *difficult*.

Stretching the kinks from her neck, Jess repositioned her hands on the steering wheel. Already that particular tension had started to twist tighter and tighter inside her and she was barely within the city limits. Her heart beat faster and her mouth grew dry.

He was here.

Memories of cruising through downtown Birmingham on hot summer nights in that convertible he'd owned back in high school rushed through her mind, doing strange things to her pulse. The lights… the stars… sitting so close to him she could feel the steady rise and fall of his chest.

She had been crazy in love with Daniel Burnett. And completely certain they would be together *forever.*

A wry laugh bubbled up in her still raw throat. "Good thing I didn't lay a wager on that one."

Ten years ago, while they were planning their wedding no less, he'd announced he couldn't be what she wanted and had come back here—to their hometown—*alone,* leaving her in Boston… *alone.*

Apparently he hadn't looked back. In fact he'd gotten married, not once but twice according to her sister, since then. The last time was scarcely a year ago. Maybe their breaking up had been a good thing.

Just hadn't felt like one at the time, or any of the other times since, whenever she'd irrationally permitted herself to wonder *what if* they'd stayed together.

Dismissing thoughts of Dan, she turned onto John Hawkins Parkway and aimed her almost new Audi toward Publix. The gently used car was a present to herself for the long awaited promotion she had worked so hard to achieve. After eight years as a special agent in the field with the Bureau, she had been selected for a rare and prestigious position at Quantico's National Center for the Analysis of Violent Crime's Behavioral Analysis Unit.

The opportunity to dissect the most evil criminal minds was both challenging and exhilarating and worth all the years of personal sacrifice. More of the images from the past thirty-six hours elbowed their way back into her thoughts.

Unable to turn off work at the end of a case much less at the end of the day.

Maybe she'd prove the shrink wrong by not allowing the carousel of cases she spent her time digging around in to haunt her last minute vacation.

Now there was a novel concept.

To her frustration, traffic was even slower moving on the parkway, but she was almost there. She worked at relaxing, first her neck and shoulders, then her arms and hands. All she had to do was let go of all things related to work.

This break would be fun. Visiting Lily and her cute little family was always a joy. Except for the blatant matchmaking. Jess rolled her eyes. Her sister was desperate to get her home permanently. Nearly all the emails she got from Lil these days included a bio on some newly divorced or widowed member of her church.

"Not going to happen, sis." Jess was never coming back here permanently.

N.E.V.E.R.

After cruising the rows of cars, she finally found a vacant slot in the crowded lot and parked. Her body complained as she unfastened her seatbelt. A fringe benefit of driving for twelve hours with only two brief stops, not to mention all the bruises she'd sustained last night joined the protest. Nothing a couple of long hot baths wouldn't fix.

The last time she'd come to Birmingham—had it been four years?—she had taken a commercial flight. Not this time. She'd needed those long driving hours alone to evict work from her head. Not an easy task for someone so hyper focused.

Well, not today. Today she wasn't a special agent with the FBI, she was Jessie Lee Harris, the sister who'd come home for Christmas.

Despite the cold, blustery weather it was considerably warmer here than the winter storm conditions she'd left back in Virginia. The streets were free of ice and snow. The only precipitation she'd run into as she crossed into Alabama was rain. She grabbed her coat and shouldered into it, then cinched the belt at her waist. The black wool blocked the crisp wind and helped to conceal her travel wrinkled clothes.

She hit the clicker, securing her car, as she headed for the entrance. "One pecan pie coming up."

While she was at it, she might just get two desserts, the promised pecan pie for tomorrow and one of those decadent hot fudge pies for tonight. Maybe she'd pick up some wine too. After the minister's son was gone and the kiddies were in bed, she, Lil, and her husband, Blake, could share a few toasts. There was plenty to celebrate. Lily had the husband, kids, and the white picket fence she had always wanted. And Jess had the promotion she'd worked so very hard to achieve.

"Careful what you wish for."

CHAPTER TWO

TWO DAYS EARLIER...
QUANTICO, VIRGINIA, 10:50 A.M.

"Harris, I'm not going to beat around the bush here."

Even before being assigned to his unit, Jess had worked with Supervisory Special Agent Gant on occasion so she wasn't exactly worried about why he'd called her into his office or about his direct tone. Going straight for the heart of the matter was his usual style. He evidently saved all his charm—assuming he had any—for civilians.

Charm or no, Jess liked him. "That saves us both some time, sir," she agreed. "I have a stack of cases waiting on my desk." Two months in the Behavioral Analysis Unit and she was either Miss Popular or simply low profiler on the food chain and got the cases no one else wanted. Didn't bother her one little bit. She was more than happy to have a crack at the most challenging subjects.

Gant leaned back in his functional, government-issue chair. It squeaked. "You were handpicked to join this unit because when it comes to ferreting out an unsub you're the best we've seen in a long time. Your instincts are spot on, Harris. Most agents can't boast about solving the cases assigned to them in any given year, much less those assigned over their career to date. You have a perfect record."

If he was hoping to butter her up, he was off to a stellar start. Jess beamed a smile. "Thank you, sir."

"Don't thank me yet." He studied her for a beat or two "I'm sure you're familiar with the Zip Code Killer."

Who wasn't? "Agent Taylor did the profile on that case last month."

She would've given her first born for that assignment—not that she had any prospects of marriage much less children—but Taylor, having moved to BAU six months ahead of Jess, was senior so he'd landed it. The "good old boys club" remained alive and well in the Federal Bureau of Investigation. Since she wasn't a "boy," she'd had to work harder and wait longer. Case in point, she and Taylor had graduated from the academy together. Taylor was a damned fine agent but, as Gant said, her record spoke for itself. Still, Taylor had gotten the plum promotion and assignment ahead of her.

No big deal. She'd never been afraid of a little extra hard work. And patience was a virtue. That was the one thing from her southern upbringing she was immensely grateful for.

"The profile Taylor built helped Agent Bedford and local law enforcement over in Warrenton identify and arrest the unsub."

Since northern Virginia fell under the jurisdiction of the DC field office, an agent assigned there, Bedford, had contacted BAU for support. Jess hadn't worked with him before, but Bedford's reputation was well regarded.

"Can't ask for much more than that," Jess offered though she suspected more was exactly what Gant hoped to attain. She'd kept up with the case. Nothing about it had gone down the way anyone had hoped.

Gant leaned forward, his chair complained again, and braced his forearms on his desk. "The problem is everyone involved, including the Bureau, is catching hell for not finding the bodies."

Folks were most unhappy that the killer, a sixty-seven year old Caucasian, who stalked young women who rented mailboxes at the post office where he had a contract to provide janitorial services, refused to give up the locations of his victims. Melvin Aniston hadn't said a single word since he was captured. Total silence.

Five young women had gone missing. The remains of one had been discovered on the property where Aniston lived. The others were presumed dead based on the length of time missing and photos found at the Aniston residence that showed the women caged, their bodies obviously abused. The families of those missing victims were left without

11

closure. Christmas was only a couple days away and the community of Warrenton, Virginia, wanted a miracle.

Miracles weren't Jess's specialty but she was damned good with murder. She was itching to get a shot at nosing around in the case.

"You may also be aware there's a witness, Delia Potter. We've kept her name and her relationship with Aniston out of the news to protect her."

"Yes, sir." Jess had heard about her all right. "She was pivotal to the investigation."

Delia Potter, not Taylor or anyone in the field conducting the investigation, was the reason the unsub had been identified. Without Potter's cooperation, Aniston might still be out there, stalking his next victim. The first of the women who'd gone missing, Shawna Johnston, had disappeared seven months ago. Larissa Stone vanished two months after that. Then Aniston suddenly got brave. His next two victims, Bonita and Marie Duncan, sisters, went missing the same day just three months ago. Victim number five, Valerie Prince, had disappeared a mere two weeks later.

No ransom demands. No bodies. No nothing. Just gone.

Until Delia Potter came forward the case had been at a standstill. She'd found photos in Aniston's house. Those photos had led to a search warrant and a veritable lottery windfall of evidence. Valerie Prince's remains had been stashed in the man's smoke house. No forensic evidence was discovered to corroborate the other four had ever been at Aniston's home. But hair and clothing fibers in the cargo area of his Subaru linked him to two more of the missing women.

They had him on one count of murder and four kidnapping charges. The death penalty was looming large. Still, the man said not a word. He had no intention of giving up the location of the other victims not even if it meant he kept breathing.

"The situation is a delicate one," Gant confessed. "Potter knows she'll be called as a witness at trial and she's not a happy camper. Trouble is, it could be years before this case goes to trial. These families deserve to know what happened to their loved ones." Gant shook his head, his expression grim. "The evidence proves he took those women—or at least was involved—but we can't say for sure if they're dead or alive. They could be dying at this very moment because their only connection to food and water is in custody."

Unless Aniston had an accomplice.

Taylor had created the profile on the unsub and advised on a course of action for those investigating the case. Bedford and the locals had turned Warrenton upside down in an attempt to find the missing women. Hotlines were still open for anyone who might have information.

No one wanted a sociopath like Aniston to get away with one final blow by refusing to give up the location of his other victims.

"Are we taking another stab at getting more information from Potter or from Aniston?" Jess crossed her legs to prevent her heel from tapping with her mounting anticipation. She would love the opportunity to square this for all involved.

If—enormous if—those women were still alive, they needed rescuing. If they weren't, the families deserved the opportunity to provide a proper burial. Jess wanted a chance to make one or the other happen.

"Aniston's not going to talk." Gant heaved an exasperated breath. "Agent Bedford believes Potter knows more than she's shared so far. Taylor agrees. I spoke with the lead detective and the prosecutor. We're all on the same page. You," Gant set his full attention on Jess, "might be able to connect with Potter. You're not a field agent anymore, Harris, but I need you to make this happen."

Jess barely suppressed the urge to jump up and do a little victory dance. "Is there reason to believe Potter might be an accomplice?"

Gant mulled over her question. "That's a possibility but no evidence has been found linking her to the women. No proof she was aware of Aniston's activities."

Something else for Jess to find out. "Will I be working with local law enforcement?"

Jurisdiction belonged to local law enforcement. At times the situation could prove a little prickly. She'd learned long ago that a thick skin was far more practical than a large ego. Rescuing or recovering the victims and solving the case were always the top priorities. As a profiler the goal was the same, she just tackled the case from a different angle with someone else doing the legwork. But she had plenty of experience in the field. If a road trip and an interview were in order, she was game.

Gant shook his head. "We've all agreed, this is your show, Harris. I want you to talk to Potter one-on-one. She's a woman, you're a woman. That could make all the difference."

Funny how being a woman suddenly mattered in the grand scheme of things. "I appreciate the opportunity to help, sir."

"Your interview skills were one of your strongest assets in the field," Gant commented. "I'm convinced you're just what we need to give these families the closure they deserve."

"I'll set up an appointment with Ms. Potter right now." Jess stood. "For today if possible."

"I was hoping you'd say that." Gant pushed to his feet. "With the holidays I wasn't sure about your plans."

She smiled. "Work is my plan, sir."

Gant cocked an eyebrow. "You and I should talk about that. Soon. We all need a vacation from time to time, Harris. Even those who aspire to be super heroes."

Her smile widened. "Thank you, sir. I'll take that as a compliment."

Warrenton, Virginia, 3:30 p.m.

Jess banged on the rickety door a third time before a female voice shouted for her to come in. There had been no answer at the house so Jess had moseyed on around to the garage turned workshop in the backyard. The car registered to Potter had been in the driveway. Made sense she was around here somewhere.

Grasping the knob, Jess gave it a twist. The door opened with hardly any effort. Inside, the pump and churn of a potter's wheel provided background noise to the fifty-three year old woman's deft hands on the clay. Jess couldn't help wondering if the lady had chosen her occupation because of her name. Maybe it was a family trade handed down through the generations.

Delia Potter was unmarried and had no children. A former school bus driver, she had been unemployed for the past fourteen months. Her personal life was littered with a history of bad luck with men. When it came to relationships, it seemed as though dear old Delia got the short end of the stick every time.

"Ms. Potter?" Jess didn't really have to ask. She recognized the woman from the photo in the case file. The blond hair surely came from a package and the inordinately pale skin suggested she preferred passing the time with indoor activities versus those done outdoors. She was tall and thin. Nothing at all like the dark, brooding man with whom she'd kept company before he was arrested for the murder of Valerie Prince and the abduction of four other young women less than half his age.

"I told the others all I know." Potter's hands glided over the wet clay, molding what appeared to be a vase. Her white tee-shirt and plaid apron was splattered with specks of clay. The jeans and sneakers she wore had seen better days. "I have nothing else to say," she added.

Potter had said the same thing when Jess called before driving the forty-five miles over here. Hadn't put Jess off in the least. People changed their minds all the time. She was counting on human nature. "I understand how you feel."

Potter glanced at her but only for a second or two. Jess walked closer, pretending to be mesmerized by her work.

A half a minute or so of silence elapsed. If asked, most anyone would say that half a minute—thirty seconds—was nothing. But when the stakes were this high, it felt like an eternity. Ticked off like hours. During that time the images of the five young women Aniston had abducted sifted one after the other through Jess's mind.

Potter was the first to break. "I don't know what you want from me."

Jess had spent the drive over here hashing out a scenario on how to approach the woman. "I want to protect *you*, Ms. Potter."

She eyed Jess warily. "You mean the way your friends at the FBI did? They promised me I wouldn't have to worry and now I find out I have to be a witness for the prosecution." She withdrew her foot from the pedal. The wheel stopped and she squashed the wet clay, jamming her fist into the long slender neck of the vase. "I don't need any more of that kind of help."

"You know how men are," Jess said with a little laugh. "No offense to my colleagues, but I do things a little different from them. When I say I want to protect you, I mean I actually have a plan that will do just that. There's no need for you to fear the next phase of this case. You did your part already. You're the hero in all this. They don't see it but I do. I can help you, Ms. Potter. I want to make this right."

She grabbed a towel and scrubbed at her hands. "I'm listening."

"You help me find where he kept the women—"

"If I knew where he kept them," Potter interrupted, throwing the towel against the damp pile of clay she'd mangled, "I would have said so right from the beginning." She planted her hands on her hips. "*If* I had known where they were, I'd be in a cell right next to Melvin. The only thing I'm guilty of is picking the wrong guy just like every other time I've trusted a man."

"I realize how hard this must be," Jess went on. "You trusted him and he took advantage of you. But I'll bet if you really think about it, you'll remember some place Melvin liked to go. Maybe some place he mentioned in the past few months. He may have had a workshop or a storage rental. He doesn't own any property other than his residence here in Warrenton but there might be another house he rented. Could be in a neighboring town or just down the street."

When Potter continued to glare at her, Jess took a chance. "The truth is, Ms. Potter, we're never going to stop looking. When we find them—and we will find them—that's when the real trouble for you will start. What you may have known will come into question all over again." The other woman's gaze narrowed. "Anything at all you might forget to mention now could come back to haunt you later."

"I said I don't know anything else. Why won't you leave me alone?" Potter crossed her arms over her chest. "I just want to be left alone."

Jess gave her a second to calm down. "That's a real shame." She sighed. "What my colleagues may have failed to tell you is if we knew where the women were or where Aniston might have held them for a time, there'd probably be a lot of evidence that directly connects him to all four. With that much evidence we wouldn't need a witness at all. There wouldn't be any reason to even mention your name since his attorney would be begging the prosecutor for a deal to avoid the death penalty."

This wasn't exactly something the Bureau could offer. In fact, Jess was making it up as she went along. But the scenario she suggested was a logical one. With enough evidence, witnesses weren't needed. They were considered unreliable more often than not. She'd certainly heard enough attorneys say as much.

Interest stirred in the other woman's eyes. "You're saying if I could help you find some more evidence—not saying I could, mind you—I could wash my hands of this whole mess?"

Jess smiled. "That's exactly what I'm saying, Ms. Potter. You help me find the place where Melvin took those girls after he snatched them and I'll make sure you don't have to show your face in the courtroom when he goes on trial."

With the right evidence there was a chance a trial wouldn't even be necessary. And if Potter turned out to be Aniston's accomplice, she wouldn't be showing her face at his trial.

She would have her own.

CHAPTER THREE

CHRISTMAS EVE

PUBLIX, HOOVER, ALABAMA, 6:45 P.M.

No hot fudge pies.

Jess scowled as she circled the festive holiday stands in the bakery section of the store for the third time.

Dozens of pies. Chocolate—not the same as hot fudge at all—apple, pecan, pecan, pecan, key-lime, peach, pumpkin.

"Shoot." Plain old chocolate would just have to do.

Jess added a chocolate pie to the basket hanging on her elbow then went in search of the wine aisle.

"Merry Christmas, shoppers," echoed from the store's intercom system.

Knowing what the coming announcement would likely be, she picked up her pace, zigzagging faster through the crowd that seemed to multiply the closer she got to the wine and beer aisle.

"Just a friendly reminder," the disembodied voice went on, "that Publix will be closing in fifteen minutes so our employees may spend the holiday with their families. Please proceed to the checkout counters with your final purchases. Thank you for shopping at Publix."

Jess cut around and between other customers as she scanned the wine labels. Something light and crisp would go well with the chocolate pie. She grabbed a bottle of Sauvignon Blanc and headed for the checkout counters.

Every register had a line of customers waiting. Jess groaned. *She was never getting out of here.* The express lines were the longest but, like her, the customers queued there had the fewest items. She made her way through the cluster and got in the shortest of the three lines. Should move reasonably quickly, she hoped.

Her cell chimed that tinkling melody. Probably Lil checking up on her again. Jess fished for her phone deep in her purse. One of these days she had to organize this hobo style handbag or get something larger. Everyday she seemed to carry more of her life around with her. Possibly, she admitted, because she was never home.

She flipped open the phone and greeted her sister. "I'm at the register now, Lil."

The woman in front of Jess glanced back at her. She smiled and shrugged. So she'd lied. Just because there were... eight, nine... ten people ahead of her didn't change the fact that she was at the register prepared for checkout. The nosy woman turned her attention forward once more.

Merry Christmas to you, too, Jess mused.

Lil's voice dragged her attention back to the phone. "You need what?" Her weary shoulders sagged as her sister lamented the fact that she'd forgotten to pick up carrots for Santa's reindeer.

For Pete's sake. How old were kids these days before they figured out Santa was just leverage their parents used to make them behave. She heaved a sigh. Oh well, it was Christmas. She should be thankful her sister wasn't ranting at her for holding up dinner.

"No problem. I'll get carrots for Rudolph and Dasher and the rest. Be there in a few." Jess shoved her phone into her purse and took a long look around the store without moving from her spot in the ever-shortening line.

Where the heck was the produce department?

"It's that way," the meddlesome lady in front of her said.

Jess forced a happy holidays smile. "Thank you."

Oh well, surely the line would be even shorter five minutes from now. The store was closing. Yeah, right. Hordes of shoppers were hastily maneuvering their carts toward the front of the store.

At the produce section, she surveyed the long tables mounded with fruits and vegetables. The cooler displays were arranged with sparkly snowflakes hanging above the apples, oranges, lettuce, tomatoes and... *carrots.*

She passed over the generic bags of baby carrots for a bunch of long carrots with the greens still attached.

"Looks like reindeer food to me." She added those to her basket.

"Jess?"

A shiver, followed immediately by a flash of heat, swept through her. Her heart thumped hard as she turned toward the man who had spoken.

Dan.

When her gaze landed on him some part of her psyche surrendered just a little bit to the weight of the past few days, as if just seeing him had pushed the load beyond what she could bear.

Good sense promptly took a hiatus and her brain immediately went into inventory mode. First of her own unkempt appearance as if she were hovering overhead, staring at her travel worn self. Her slacks were wrinkled from all those hours behind the wheel. The matching black sweater had a speck of mustard on the front from the burger she'd gotten at a drive through just this side of Roanoke. At least her coat covered that unsightly mess. The burn in her cheeks warned her face had just gone bright red.

More disconcerting than all that combined, she hadn't bothered with makeup and her hair, which hadn't seen a brush since sometime after midnight, was in a ponytail.

She looked like hell.

He, on the other hand, looked amazing.

Before her brain could kick back into gear and organize the proper verbal response, he hugged her. Her lungs filled with the scent of him... he smelled like rain... fresh and clean with a hint of that same sexy aftershave he'd worn when they were together.

He released her. She swayed before she could recapture her equilibrium. "Dan." She gave a nervous laugh as she glanced around, hoping against hope this was some sort of delusion brought on by the stress she'd come here to escape. "Of all things... running into you *here*."

There had to be a hundred supermarkets in the Birmingham area. What were the odds?

There was only one possible answer. God was getting back at her for leaving Him behind along with Santa Claus at the ripe old age of ten. Who wanted to believe in anything when your parents suddenly died on you and a foster home became your new address?

Not Jessie Lee Harris. She hadn't believed in anything but work since.

Maybe she hadn't believed sufficiently in the man staring at her right now to salvage their relationship as it fell apart ten years ago.

No. He was the one who walked out. *He left her.*

As if ten years hadn't passed, the compulsion to slap his face abruptly expanded inside her. Just as suddenly, the impulse to cry washed it away.

What in the world had she been thinking coming here?

It wasn't bad enough that the preacher's son waited for her at Lil's house, she'd just run into her first and only love in Publix when she looked her absolute worst.

Determination surged, chasing away all those other frustrating emotions. She would not permit an up close encounter with the past to make a fool of her.

She opened her mouth to say something witty then snapped it shut. He was staring at her. She might have been offended except he was smiling. Much to her irritation, her entire being reacted to that gorgeous smile. And those incredible blue eyes. No man had a right to look that good. His dark hair was a little longer. He hadn't shaved in days and still he took her breath away.

She should have gone for another of those psych evaluations instead of coming here. Maybe even paid attention.

Dan shook his head. "I can't believe you're here."

That was a cue for her to speak. Where was all that bravado now, Jess? "I'm headed to my sister's," she blurted. "For Christmas."

Just die right here and now. Of course she was here for Christmas and headed to her sister's. Why oh why did she have to embarrass herself in front of him of all people?

More of that thick, consuming silence lapsed between them with him staring at her as if he didn't know what to say next.

She certainly didn't. She'd said too much already.

Years... she hadn't seen Daniel Burnett in almost ten years. Yet, he looked exactly the same, maybe better. He'd filled out a little. Broad shoulders looked even broader in that navy suit jacket. The tee shirt beneath gave a nice preview of just how well he'd kept in shape. Jeans hugged the rest of him. She wasn't even going there.

No question about it, thirty-something looked good on him.

Thirty-something, on the other hand, had done nothing kind for her. She rarely found time for the gym. Forgot to eat more often than not. He was probably staring at her trying to figure out what happened to the cute blond he used to know.

You're not supposed to care, Jess. Except she did.

"Oh man." He gave his head a little shake as if he was still having trouble believing his eyes. "I'll have to thank my mother tomorrow."

"Your mother?" Confusion, then disdain marred Jess's brow before she could stop it. Katherine Burnett had always hated her. *Always.* From her first date with Dan, his mother had decided Jess wasn't good enough for her only son.

"She makes a sweet potato casserole every year for Christmas dinner," he explained, "but this year she forgot one essential ingredient." He held up a clear plastic bag containing four large sweet potatoes. "I almost forgot to stop. And here you are."

Somehow she kept her smile in place while her lips tried their level best not to tremble. "Here I am."

"This might sound crazy," he began, "but... we really need to catch up. Have a drink or something."

Panic tightened around her throat, cutting off her ability to breathe and reminding her it was still raw from last night. "Lil's expecting me."

Could her voice sound any shakier? Not to mention she'd already told him she was headed to her sister's.

"An hour." Dan reached for her basket. "I haven't seen you in forever." His fingers brushed hers as he took the load from her. She trembled in spite of her best efforts. "Come on, Jess. Lil will understand. Just one hour. For old time's sake."

If he hadn't looked so sincere... if her brain hadn't gone to mush... maybe she might have been able to marshal up a no rather than going with what could surely only be morbid curiosity.

"Sure." She swallowed at the massive lump of unstable emotions in her throat. "For old time's sake."

That breath-stealing smile of his was nearly enough to banish all the reasons this was a colossal mistake. *You are in serious trouble here, Jess.*

As he ushered her toward the row of checkout lines at the front of the store, she kept her lips sealed tight to hold back the bout of hysterical laughter building inside her.

It was a miracle she had survived the past twenty-four hours.

Now her sister was going to kill her.

CHAPTER FOUR

"I thought staying the night would be prudent," Jess explained to her boss. Calling in this morning was essential since she'd opted to stay in the field and follow up with Delia Potter.

As he rambled on about the case, she sipped her coffee and surveyed the snowy parking lot outside the IHOP. The white stuff had started coming down hard as she'd driven away from the meeting with Potter late yesterday afternoon. With every radio station she perused forecasting a possible ten to twelve inches of snow overnight, staying put had seemed the best plan. Considering the Christmas rush would only add to potential travel issues, she hadn't wanted to take any chances.

Sunrise had confirmed she'd made the right decision. The roads were a mess. Since Delia Potter planned a trip to Cincinnati this afternoon to spend the holidays with her family, catching her this morning was imperative.

Jess glanced at the sky. Puffy white clouds with a hint of gray threatened more of the same. She wondered how many flights would be cancelled. Potter might not be going anywhere after all. Jess was a little surprised she'd been able to obtain permission from the local authorities for the travel despite the ongoing investigation. A quick call to the lead detective who didn't understand Jess's surprise had confirmed Potter's assertion. It was, after all, almost Christmas, he'd reminded her.

As long as she got what she needed from the lady before she left town, Jess would be happy. She was on the case now and she wasn't about to allow this to be the one she failed to wrap up with a nice, neat bow.

"What's your take on Potter?" Gant wanted to know. "You get the feeling she knows more than she's shared so far?" He didn't bother trying to camouflage the hope in his voice.

Any margin for optimism was minimal at this stage but what little there was Jess owned it. Delia Potter had asked her to come back this morning. She had presented the impression she wanted to talk but said she needed time to think. Not exactly an appropriate reaction for someone who had nothing else to say and nothing to hide.

Jess had spent last night going over the case file Gant had provided and mulling over the meeting with Potter. The woman had exhibited no apparent discomfort during their brief conversation, at least not once she got passed the I-don't-want-to-go-to-court attitude. Her demeanor suggested reluctance and impatience. What the woman really wanted was off the hook with her former lover's troubles.

"I think," Jess weighed her words carefully, "Delia Potter believes she knows something relevant but doesn't want to get mired any deeper than she already is."

Gant hummed a noncommittal note. "I'm counting on you, Harris. Chances are those women are dead. I have no illusions this is going to have a happy ending. Either way, we need to know what he did with them."

"I'll do what I can," Jess assured him again.

Delia Potter walked in. She looked from one booth to the next.

"She's here. I'll call when I have something."

Jess shoved the phone into her purse and waved. Potter strolled toward the table, her stride unhurried. She set her purse on the brown faux leather and removed her coat before scooting into the booth.

"I'm glad you could make it." Jess gifted her with a smile as she motioned for the waitress.

Potter ordered coffee, then announced, "I want this over. No offense to you, Agent Harris, but I don't want any more visits from cops. I'd like to move on with my life."

"I can certainly understand." There were four families out there who wanted their loved ones back.

Jess had no sympathy for the woman but it was best not to mention as much.

The waitress dropped off a fresh carafe of coffee and moved on to the next table.

"This might be nothing," Potter began, "but it's been nagging at me."

"The smallest detail might be just the one we need," Jess prompted.

Potter seemed to brace herself. "I didn't mention anything about Dale because it didn't seem right to burden him with all this. Frankly, I've had moments when I wished I'd just walked away and never said a word."

How selfless of her. "Who's Dale?"

"Dale Pritchard. He was in Nam with Melvin. They were prisoners of war together. Shared the same cage." She shook her head. "You have no idea what those two suffered. The stories Melvin told me." She shuddered. "I can't help wondering if that's what turned him into what he is today."

Jess had read Aniston's file. He was a decorated veteran. Despite being a POW, there was no history of diagnosed or treated post-traumatic stress disorder in his file. No history of any sort of trouble, legal or otherwise. Those who knew him considered him a nice, quiet man who kept to himself. Evidently Aniston's still waters ran deeper than anyone suspected.

"Does Dale live in Warrenton?"

Potter cradled her coffee with both hands. "He lives on the other side of Ruckersville. About an hour and a half from here. Dale doesn't get out much. He spends most of his time in a wheelchair nowadays. Like I said, they both came back from Nam in bad shape. I guess I just didn't want to see how bad."

"The two kept in touch?" Jess's instincts had started to buzz.

Potter nodded. "Melvin has visited Dale about once a month for as long as I've known him."

Nothing particularly suspicious about visiting a war buddy. "Do you believe Melvin may have shared information with Dale about the women?"

Potter stared at her coffee for a moment. "I honestly don't know," she took a big breath, "but about six months ago he started spending a lot more time with Dale. Going over a couple of times a week. I guess I got a little jealous. Seemed like he was never around for me anymore."

Now they were getting somewhere. "Did you ask about this sudden change? Maybe his friend was sick and needed his attention?"

"He wouldn't talk about it. Said it was none of my business."

"Have you contacted Dale since Melvin's arrest?" Aniston was taken into custody three weeks ago. Surely the other man had wondered what was going on, whether he watched the news or not. "Has Dale called to see why Melvin hasn't visited him lately?"

"That's what got me to thinking." She set her coffee down and leaned toward Jess, her face a study in concern. "He hasn't called or anything. I guess that was the part that started to nag at me. It didn't feel right."

"Does Dale live alone? He may be ill." Or dead. If there was no one to check on him anything could have happened. "Have you attempted to get in touch with him?"

"I tried to call but he didn't answer." She frowned and shifted in her seat as if growing uncomfortable. "Melvin told me once that no one knew him the way Dale did. I'm worried now that Dale figured out what Melvin was doing and he did something awful to him."

Jess took a pad and pencil from her purse. "Write down Dale's address and phone number and I'll check on him. See what I can find out for you."

Potter glanced out the window. "His place is off the main highway. You might have trouble getting to him if this weather keeps up."

Abrupt winter storms were just something you got used to in northern Virginia. Jess had learned to be prepared. Boots and a blanket in the trunk along with a change of clothes and a spare toothbrush. Her work took her away from home regularly, being equipped for an overnighter was just part of the job. Since moving to BAU she'd missed the field work. Maybe that was part of the reason she'd stayed last night. It felt good to be back in the game at this level.

"You just enjoy the holiday with your family, Ms. Potter. I'll get an update on Dale." Jess studied the older woman as she jotted down the information. "Is there anything else you remembered?"

Potter passed the notepad and pencil back to Jess. "Nothing." She sighed, more of that worry in her expression. "I hope I'm not wasting your time. Dale's sixty-eight and his health isn't very good. I keep wondering if maybe I made a mistake by not mentioning him sooner. If he's part of this, those women could all be dead because of me."

Interesting about face from yesterday's attitude. Her tone and demeanor appeared genuine. Maybe too much so. Jess offered a sympathetic smile. "You did remember and that's what matters. After I've paid Dale a visit, how about I give you a call and let you know how he's doing?"

Potter looked relieved. She pressed a hand to her chest. "That would be so thoughtful of you. Are you going today? I can call him again. Leave a message. He always checks his machine."

Really? But just a few minutes ago she claimed to have tried calling Dale and he hadn't answered. Why hadn't she left a message if he always checked his machine?

"Yes, I'm going today." Jess finished off her coffee. "I'll drive over as soon as we're finished here. Why don't I take your sister's name and number? You said she's in Cincinnati? What time's your flight again?"

Jess had a feeling Ms. Delia Potter was planning a disappearing act of her own.

CHAPTER FIVE

Cops and lawyers. Even on Christmas Eve the downtown pub was filled with people who either hunted down the bad guys or prosecuted them. Jess didn't remember this place from before. Then again, it was a little more upscale than the places they had stolen into as teenagers.

The building was an old one with a lot of the historic architectural details still intact. The decor was stark and urban. But the crowd was warm and friendly. Jess couldn't deny an instant kinship.

"So you work for the mayor?" She traced the sweat sliding down her longneck bottle of beer. There was nothing particularly unique about the domestic label but it gave her a distraction. Every time she settled her gaze on Dan she got lost somehow.

"I'm the liaison between the mayor's office and the police department. It's a new position. One we've needed for years."

36

"You're turning into a politician after all." She'd always said he would make a good one. He could charm anyone into most anything.

Dan laughed. "I don't know about that but I do enjoy my work. It gives me an opportunity to make a difference, you know what I mean?"

She gave a nod. "I absolutely do."

Her gaze rested back on the bottle. It was better than looking into the mirror behind the bar. On the drive from Publix she'd dragged the ponytail holder from her hair and run her brush through it. Three Altoids had numbed her tongue but at least she'd gotten the too-many-hours-on-the-road taste out of her mouth.

Dan had offered to drive her but there was no way she was getting into his vehicle alone with him. No way.

Speaking of his ride. "What happened to the Thunderbird?" The convertible he'd driven all through high school and college had been replaced by a big Chevy SUV. A nice ride but not nearly as sexy. Not a *Dan* car.

He grinned. "You always did like that car."

She would be lying if she denied the charge. They'd made love for the first time in the backseat. "I guess I did."

He looked away but not before she saw the flash of guilt in his eyes. "It was time to get something more reliable. The T-Bird had a lot of miles on it." He knocked back a slug of his beer.

She supposed that was his way of saying he'd needed to move on. Why not? He'd certainly moved on from her in all other ways. Jess turned up her beer to drown the thought. What the hell was she doing? She felt like one of those people who couldn't stop staring at the steam rising from the mangled metal of the two cars that had just collided.

"You've certainly moved up from that Jetta you drove all over Boston."

Jess set the beer aside and plucked a peanut from the small bowl the bartender and provided. "It was time." She'd practically driven the wheels off that old Jetta.

Unlike the Thunderbird, they hadn't made love in her Jetta. Instead, they'd spent most of their time in it quarreling. She would never forget the first time she'd left Boston headed to Quantico for a summer internship with the Bureau. Dan hadn't made the list. They'd spent most of the summer apart. If she hadn't been so focused on making an impression, she would have realized that was the beginning of the end.

They'd argued before she'd driven away. He insisted he wanted her to go and yet she had sensed his emotional withdrawal. Barely a year later he was ready to come back to Alabama without her. Only when he'd driven away there hadn't been any arguing. There hadn't even been a goodbye.

She tossed the nut back in the bowl and finished off her beer. "This was fun." *Not.* "I should get going."

He couldn't let her go.

"I saw Lil a few weeks ago," Dan interjected, hoping to distract her from leaving. Not that he could blame her. He'd said all the wrong things. He'd definitely made all the wrong moves.

Maybe it was the shock of seeing her after all this time. He couldn't believe she was here. She was still just as beautiful as the first time he'd laid eyes on her at that football game. His first thought had been of how very much he'd wanted her.

"You did?" Jess looked surprised. "Lil didn't mention it."

He loved her eyes. They were the deepest brown. The rich dark color was a vivid contrast to her creamy skin and lush blonde hair. God, he'd dreamed of that face so many times.

"Where did you see her?"

Pay attention, man. "Her son was one of twenty students to receive an academic commendation from the mayor. He's a smart kid."

"Both her kids are smart." Jess smiled. "Lil and Blake are doing a great job as parents."

Dan's chest tightened. He couldn't help wondering if he and Jess had stayed together if they would have had kids by now. Not likely. She was too career oriented. He glanced at her ring finger again. He wondered why there wasn't at least an engagement ring there.

He, on the other hand, had muddled his way through two marriages. Both had been mistakes. He flinched. Not a subject he wanted to visit tonight.

Another thing he didn't want right now was to spend just one hour with this woman. He wanted to know everything about her. Sixty minutes would never be enough.

When she reached for her purse, he said the first thing that came to mind, "You still have that apartment?"

She jerked her head up as if he'd shouted. "No... I have a condo, but I'm looking for a house in Stafford since I'm in Virginia now."

Felt strange to think of her living some place besides that apartment... the one they had shared. "I just got a place downtown. I'm on call twenty-four/ seven, living in the heart of the city seemed like the smart way to go."

Her smile slipped a little. She was ready to go. His gut clenched. What did he expect? That she'd be happy to see him?

Not after he'd walked away... even he hadn't for-given himself for that one. Maybe he never would.

A new kind of hope flared inside him. This was his chance. Maybe running into each other had been fate. He had a chance to set things to rights between them.

"My new place is just across the street," he said quickly. "You have to see the view. You'll love it. I swear."

Her posture changed, stiffened. Those dark eyes turned wary. She was going to say no. "Dan, that's—"

"An excellent idea." He stood and reached for her hand. "Remember, I have connections in this town. Give me any trouble, Agent Harris, and I might have to pull some strings."

She laughed. The rich sound made his heart glad. How he had missed her laugh.

"Five minutes," she warned, "and then I'm on my way."

"Deal."

He'd negotiated himself a few more minutes. Now all he had to do was find the guts to say what needed to be said before his time was up.

CHAPTER SIX

Jess slowed her Audi and stared at the road sign. It was an old one, part of the lettering was worn off. *G..en . . .f.* Looked like Green Leaf to her. Potter said she'd only been here once but the old farmhouse was at the end of Green Leaf Road just off Route 610.

"Hope this is you, Mr. Pritchard."

She would have been here an hour ago if not for a damned flat tire. After Delia Potter headed for the airport, Jess was stuck at the IHOP until Warrenton Tire & Auto could get someone over to remedy the situation. As she made the turn onto Green Leaf, she hoped there was a gravel road beneath this blanket of fluff. Fortunately, all the main roads had been cleared. But not the side roads like this one. She glanced up at the sky. The white stuff was still coming down. Was it getting heavier now? She hoped not.

The farther she drove down the narrow road the more the woods seemed to close in on it. Drifts of snow perched on every available ledge. The evergreen branches were loaded down with it reminding her that Christmas was only two days away. Lil had been begging her to come home for the holidays. Thanksgiving hadn't happened and now she was pushing for Christmas. It had been a long time.

But holidays were just like any other day for Jess. She didn't even bother with a tree. She was never home anyway. The few times a year when she saw her family they came to Virginia.

Lil never let too much time pass between visits and she didn't understand why it had to be work first with Jess.

This case was a perfect example. It couldn't wait. Even so guilt was her constant companion. Particularly when she had no choice but to disappoint her sister each time she asked. There simply was no other way. Christmas or not, the important thing right now was finding answers for the families of the victims in this case.

This lead might not pan out but there was only one way to find out. Jess dug out her cell and put through another call to Gant. She'd called twice already and he'd been in a meeting. Taylor had apparently been in the same meeting. She hadn't wanted to leave a message for Gant until she had something he didn't know already. Another glance at the sky warned that, at this point, she just needed someone to know where she was.

Gant's voice rattled across the line, the sound going in and out. Jess checked the bars on her screen. "Dammit." Only one. She braked to a stop, causing the car to skid a little. She held her breath until it stilled.

"Harris?"

"Sorry about that," she said to Gant. "I had to stop, the reception is really, really bad."

"Where… you?"

He was breaking up. Hopefully he could hear better on his end. "I'm following up on a lead Delia Potter gave me. A Dale Pritchard. He and Aniston were POWs together in Vietnam."

Gant was shouting unintelligible words at her again.

"I'm at a farm on Green Leaf Road off Route 610 near Ruckersville. Green Leaf Road," she repeated. "Off 610."

"I don't like this… ready… me."

Frustration shortened her patience. He sends her to learn what no one else had and now he says he doesn't like this. "I can't hear you." She repeated the address a third time and ended the call. There was nothing else to do. If Pritchard had a landline, she would call Gant from there. Hopefully he was expecting her. Potter had said she would try to reach him.

"Ready or not." Jess resumed her journey.

The old farmhouse sat in a clearing at least a mile off the main road. An old pickup truck was parked next to the house. A barn was visible near the tree line. Not much else around but woods and snow.

"Fun. Fun." She turned off the engine and reached into the passenger floorboard for her boots. She'd had the foresight to get them out of the trunk this morning.

When she climbed out of the car the snow almost reached the tops of her boots. She grimaced. Cold feet were bad enough. If the snow got into her boots, cold, *wet* feet would be way worse. Before closing her door she tucked her Glock into her coat pocket... just in case.

That was the thing about having spent eight years in the field, you learned to buy the right clothes. No shallow pockets. No thick, lined gloves either. The thinner, formfitting kind kept her hands warm enough and allowed for a good grip on her weapon.

She trudged the short distance to the porch steps. The snow crunching under her boots was the only sound. Spooky quiet. Three steps up and she was on the porch. The faintest whistling of wind through the trees whirred in the air.

Jess scanned the area again. The truck hadn't moved since the big snow dump last night. Maybe he didn't use that old truck. Could he even drive? Potter hadn't mentioned anyone else living here. Although there was a visible set of ruts where it appeared a vehicle had driven past the house some time earlier today. She couldn't accurately judge how long ago but snow was beginning to fill those tracks now.

Moving to the end of the porch, she checked the area around the barn. Nothing there either. Maybe someone had made a delivery. Or, for all she knew, Pritchard had a housekeeper or nurse. A relative may have come to take him home for the holidays.

She hoped she hadn't come all this way to find an empty house.

Jess rapped on the door. Nothing. She banged a little harder.

Still nothing.

She reached into her pocket with her right hand and curled her fingers around her Glock. "Mr. Pritchard, you in there? I'm Special Agent Jess Harris from the Federal Bureau of Investigation. Delia Potter sent me to check on you." She reached for the doorknob with her left hand. "Mr. Pritchard?"

The knob turned easily. Not locked. Braced for trouble, she stepped to the side and gave the door a shove with one booted foot. No lights on inside. "Mr. Pritchard, are you okay in there?"

Total silence was all she got for her trouble.

"Mr. Pritchard, I need to speak with you, sir." She felt on the wall by the door for a switch. Flipped it. Still no light. Either the power had gone out from the storm or the man hadn't paid his bill. Then again, could be a blown bulb. She moved a few feet deeper into the house. Pritchard was an elderly, disabled man. He could be in need of medical care, giving her reasonable cause to enter the premises.

Damn. She shivered. It was as cold in here as it was outside. There was a fireplace with enough ash to suggest someone had been burning wood but not recently.

She blinked repeatedly to help her eyes adjust faster to the dim interior as she took another step toward what she estimated to be the kitchen. "Mr. Pritchard, please call out to me if you if you can hear me. Do you need medical attention?"

The house was relatively small. Paneled walls and low ceilings with wood floors. Newspapers were stacked in a neat pile on the sofa. A half empty glass of water sat on a table next to a well-used chair. The place was as silent as a tomb.

A soft sound jerked Jess to the left, toward the far side of the living room. She aimed her weapon in that direction.

"Hello?"

The sound came again. *Help!* Too indistinct to determine if it was male or female.

"Mr. Pritchard?" Moving quickly, she entered a long narrow hallway. Three doors. Two on the left, one on the right. Bedrooms and a bath most likely. Calling for backup would be the preferred protocol about now, but there was no time. If the old man needed medical attention she was going to have a hell of a time getting him out of the house. With no cell service and no sign of a landline as of yet, she might not have a choice.

Where the hell was that phone Potter claimed he had?

The faint cry for help came again. Seemed to be coming from door number two on her left. She edged closer. Her pulse rate revved up as adrenaline pumped through her body. The door was ajar.

Leading with her Glock, she pushed the door inward. Next to the bed a man sat slumped in his wheelchair. A dark green blanket covered most of his torso.

"Mr. Pritchard?" Jess moved toward him. It was even colder in here. She crouched down to get a look at his face. "Mr. Prit—"

His face was frozen in pain... eyes wide open... mouth gaping in mid-cry. Throat slashed. Blood had soaked into the green wool of the blanket and dried. He had been dead for a while. Days, maybe a week.

Jess swore. She might as well drive back out to the main road where reception was better and call—

Something went around her neck—rope—and she was jerked backward. She scrambled to get up... to get free. She twisted, tried to get her weapon around to shoot at whoever was choking her.

The rope tightened.

A weight settled on her back, pressed her face to the floor.

Jess bucked and twisted her body to throw off the weight. Didn't work. She jabbed her elbow at her attacker. Couldn't connect. The rope grew tighter and tighter. Her weapon discharged. The room was spinning... growing darker.

No air.

CHAPTER SEVEN

"This is it." Dan grinned at her as he shoved the key into the lock. "It's not where I hope to be in a couple of years but it's home for now."

He opened the door and waited as Jess stepped into the apartment. *Dan's place.* She had lost her mind. "It's... nice."

Her body had started trembling as they walked across the street from the pub and hadn't stopped yet. Dammit. He'd have to be blind not to see. She'd mentally kicked herself at least a dozen times during the elevator ride to the eighth floor.

What was she doing?

Lil was upset. She hadn't said as much but Jess had heard it in her voice when she'd called to explain they shouldn't hold dinner for her. She'd be there in time for dessert.

What kind of sister did this make her? She hadn't bothered to come to Birmingham for a visit in over

49

four years and now that she was here she'd chosen *him* over Lil.

The man who had shattered her heart. The same one who had walked away and left Jess to pick up the pieces *alone*.

The shrinks were right. All this time the stress had been building and now she had cracked.

"I'm still not organized." Dan picked up the newspaper he'd probably left on the sofa that morning. "It's a great location." He snagged the coffee cup on the end table next. "I walk to work most days."

He stood in the middle of the room holding the newspaper and coffee mug as if he didn't know what to do next. Maybe she wasn't the only one who was nervous. Now that they were in his personal territory, his confidence seemed to slip. The idea provided a tiny fraction of relief since she had gone from shocked and unsettled to shaking and uncertain herself. And maybe just a little terrified.

All these years she'd wondered what it would be like if they ever ran into each other again. This was not how she'd pictured the meeting.

Her heart beat faster and faster. She had pretended to forget all about him. The way he smelled and tasted had been blocked to save her sanity. Every moment of the way he'd made love to her that first time—her first time—had been totally exiled. The very concept of how she had loved Daniel Burnett with her entire heart and soul had been buried.

Until now.

All of it. Every tiny detail had flooded her as she'd walked across that dark street at his side.

Oh yes. She was out of her mind.

He tossed the newspaper into a recycle bin then deposited the coffee mug on the counter near the sink.

Take a breath, Jess. Stop fixating on his every move. "That's great. The place…" she glanced around "… suits you."

He moved toward her and the breath she'd only just managed to squeeze into her lungs locked there.

"Let me take your coat."

It wasn't until he reached toward her that she snapped out of the daze she couldn't seem to shake and yanked at the belt knotted at her waist. Fingers fumbling, she wasn't having much luck.

He deftly took over, easily releasing the knot. "You must be exhausted after that drive."

"It wasn't so bad." She squeezed her hands into fists to stop their confounded shaking.

He lifted her purse from her shoulder and placed it on the sofa. "I'm glad the weather cooperated."

"That makes two of us." Somehow she managed a smile as she eased out of her coat. Her body complained, reminding her that it had taken a beating.

He draped her coat on a hook near the door and then he shouldered out of his jacket and hung it next hers. That simple action affected her somehow, made her yearn for things she would only regret wanting. This was such a bad idea.

"Good thing that snow storm the Weather Channel was taking about didn't follow you south."

"A very good thing," she agreed. The memory of falling onto her knees in the snow and staring up at the moon filled her head. She forced it away.

Before more images from the scene she'd left in Virginia could intrude, she distracted herself with taking in more details of his place. The main living area was one big room. A leather sofa, a chair and a couple of tables made up the furnishings. The décor was single male. No paintings, just a couple of family photos his mother had probably added. Of course there was a large television presiding over one corner. In sharp contrast, the kitchen was small, perfect for a bachelor or a couple. The ceiling soared to about twelve feet preventing the urban space from feeling so cramped.

But the true focal point was on the other side of the room. Massive windows looked out over the city. Memories from their shared past crowded in on her. She couldn't seem to stay focused.

"Have a seat."

She turned back to him and watched as he crossed to the kitchen. She wanted to kick herself for salivating as if she'd never seen a man walk across a room before. *You are so truly pathetic, Jess.*

"Wine?" He held up a bottle and grinned. "I was assured this Prosecco was in the top ten best wines for Christmas."

How could she say no to that hopeful face? "Sure," she relented, aware that she still had to drive to Lil's.

With yet another bad decision behind her, rather than permit herself to stand there and gawk at him, she drifted to the windows. She peered through the night and tried to make out the landmarks unique to this city.

How was it that she couldn't look at a starry Birmingham night without thinking of all those times driving through the city in that old convertible. He'd always kept one strong arm wrapped around her shoulders. She'd felt like the world was theirs and theirs alone. Anything had been possible as long as they had each other.

Sadness mushroomed so swiftly, so sharply inside her she lost her breath again. How had everything fallen apart? They'd planned their lives so carefully... where had they gone wrong?

"I know I'm repeating myself," he said as he joined her at the window, "but I can't believe you're here."

They hadn't gone wrong. He was the one who had walked away. Jess turned on him, ready to say what she'd wanted to say for years. But his smile stole her words. Or maybe it was his eyes. What a complete idiot she was. He thrust a glass at her and she took it. Wished it were a double shot of bourbon.

"It has been a long time." She kicked aside the confusing emotions and focused her attention on the spectacular view. "I've been busy." A blast of anger shored up her confidence. "I just got a big promotion. Did I mention that?"

"You look exactly the same, Jess."

Was he even listening? She wanted to rant at him.

"I can't stop staring at you," he said, his voice filled with awe.

She warned herself not to risk meeting his gaze after a statement like that but she'd never been very good at following orders, not even her own. "I hope that's a compliment."

"That's definitely a compliment." He frowned. "What's this?" He reached out with his right hand, pushed her hair back and traced the bruise at her throat.

"It's nothing." She drew away from his touch. Sipped the wine. Sweet and sparkly, the kind she liked. She'd hated wine when he'd first introduced her to it. Beer had been the illicit beverage of choice among the teenagers on her side of the tracks. He'd taken her to the best restaurants and bought her expensive gifts... and she'd fallen head over heels in love with him.

"It doesn't look like nothing," he countered.

The edge in his voice warned that he had the wrong idea. "Just a work thing. That's all."

He nodded but he looked far from convinced. She looked away. Staring at him had gotten her into trouble more than once... like when she'd lost her virginity.

Time to get this conversation back into less treacherous territory.

"You're the one who hasn't changed a bit other than you apparently lost your razor." Judging by the dark stubble on his jaw he hadn't shaved in at least a couple of days. His hair was a little longer. Daniel Burnett had always been the clean cut all-American guy. What was up with the new look? "The mayor doesn't mind that you're working so hard to resurrect that eighties unshaven look?"

"This," he laughed and scrubbed at his unshaven chin, "is my mother's doing."

Jess's self-confidence level dropped another couple of notches. Why had she asked? Katherine Burnett had never liked Jess. She doubted her opinion had changed. Since Dan was an only child, Katherine's entire existence revolved around trying to mold his life and to ensure it turned out the way *she* wanted it. Part of Jess would always believe his mother was to some degree responsible for their break up.

Ancient history.

"She staging a Christmas production for her church. I was volunteered to play Joseph. Tomorrow night's the big show."

See, Jess, his life was everything his mother had planned without you. What was she doing here?

"You know," she shoved the glass back at him, "I really should go. Lily is—"

"Please," he urged, shutting down her excuse. He stared at her lips for long enough to have her heart racing before finally lifting his gaze to hers. "I want to hear all about you and that promotion. It could be years before I see you again."

Suddenly the trouble she'd gotten herself into yesterday seemed like a walk in the park.

The only thing she'd risked then was her life.

Tonight she was risking her heart...

He had to think of a way to persuade her to stay.

What he was asking was too much, he realized that, but he couldn't help himself. He wanted to know all about her life now. His own had been so upside down the past few months he'd hardly had time to think about anything but work and the divorce.

Memories crashed against him. The gun aimed at his head... the hurt of knowing he had failed.

Not going there.

Jess was here. He couldn't believe his eyes. She was here... with him if only for a little while. He wasn't foolish enough to believe they would ever have a second chance at a life together—hers was in Virginia and he didn't see that changing—but maybe they could be friends. They'd shared too much to pretend there wasn't still some connection between them.

"Okay." She squared her shoulders and gave him a firm look. "But just this one glass of wine and then I really have to go."

The gut-wrenching tension receded. He couldn't remember the last time he'd felt that much relief.

Maybe when his ex had missed putting a bullet in his head with his own weapon.

"Then let's make it count." He tapped his glass to hers. "To a Christmas to remember."

This was the best one he'd had in a very long time.

CHAPTER EIGHT

ONE DAY EARLIER...
RUCKERSVILLE

Pain.

Jess told her eyes to open. Her throat ached. She tried to reach up and touch it but couldn't. Her arms were too heavy. There was something she needed to remember but her head felt swollen and too much like cotton. Her mouth tasted salty.

A low moan echoed around her.

Had she made that sound? Where was she?

She was supposed to...

Her eyes opened and terror detonated in her veins.

Zip Code Killer...Pritchard farm.

Dead man...wheelchair.

She tried to speak, but her mouth was stuffed with some kind of cloth. She tried to move. Couldn't. Her hands were tied behind her back. Her legs were secured at the ankles. Her body ached.

It was so cold.

Assess your surroundings.

Slowly, she quieted her breathing and let the thumping in her chest ease. The floor was cold and grimy. Not dirt or wood. It felt like concrete or maybe stone. She lay on her belly, her legs twisted to the right and her left cheek pressed against the chilly, unyielding surface. The room was dimly lit. Not the natural kind from the sun. Fluorescent lights, she decided, but not close. Across the room.

There was that sound again. Small, weak... a moan.

Rocking her body she managed to get onto her right side and raise her head. She'd expected to see stalls or farm equipment. But this didn't seem to be the barn behind the house. Not like any barn she'd ever been inside.

Basement? Maybe. The ceilings were lower than normal, six or seven feet. The walls were lined with shelves cluttered with canning jars and boxes.

Don't just lay there. Get up. Find a way to get loose.

Her mind worked a little slow, felt a little groggy. She'd been drugged, no doubt. At least she was awake. Definitely a good sign. Judging by the condition of the man in the wheelchair if whoever had attacked her wanted her dead, she would be dead.

Jess curled her knees toward her waist and rocked up onto her butt. The room did some spinning. Her stomach churned and bile roiled up into her throat. She tried to swallow it back. Puking would be a bad thing under the circumstances.

Whoever had wrapped that rope around her neck and choked her until she lost consciousness must have used a fast acting drug to keep her that way. She wouldn't have been out for so long otherwise. As sore and cold as she felt, this floor had been her bed for a couple hours anyway.

The salty taste in her mouth suggested GHB, a too frequently used date-rape drug. Worked quickly and, depending on the dose, kept the vic down for a good stretch.

Son of a bitch. Anger helped to clear her head. How the hell had her attacker sneaked up on her so easily? Had two months away from field work made her that rusty?

Let it go. Get your bearings.

All she could see from her position were the stocked shelves, a mountain of plastic containers and that fluorescent light fixture with its one working bulb. No windows and just one door.

Get up! Get out of here!

She braced for hitting the concrete face first as she attempted to shift onto her knees. With her head still reeling it wasn't an easy feat but she managed. She listened for running footsteps or shouting. With all the grunting she'd done anyone nearby would have heard her.

So far, so good.

If she could just get this rag out of her mouth. She shuddered, fought the gag reflex. That quiet moaning started again. Jess stilled, the reality finally penetrating the fog in her brain.

Someone else was here with her.

She rested on her knees and focused on recapturing her balance. When she felt steady enough, she started to scoot. As she slowly made her way across the room, she twisted her wrists and pulled at the bindings there. By the time she reached the nearest wall, her stomach was lurching again. She rested her shoulder against a shelf and gave herself a second before attempting to get to her feet.

With only one false start she was standing. She waited for the ground to stop tilting. A frown furrowed her forehead as she stared at her feet. Where were her boots? One of her socks was missing too.

So that was the rag in her mouth. At least it was her sock and not someone else's.

Another survey of the room drew her attention to the ceiling. Floor joists and those crisscross braces verified her initial assessment: basement.

When she felt confident enough, she started to hop. Three or four falls onto her knees had tears burning her eyes. She ignored the pain. Had to loosen these bindings enough to free her hands. While she was at it, she needed to find where the moaning was coming from.

Beyond the stack of plastic containers were two massive wooden posts in the middle of the room. There was a door to the left and a steep set of stairs to the right. She opted for the stairs. It was slow going but only one fall before she reached the first of the two posts that stood between her and that potential escape route.

She leaned against the post for a second. A couple of big rusty nails protruding at just about chin level gave her an idea. Not allowing herself time to think twice, she opened her mouth wide and lowered it over one of the nails, just far enough to try snagging the sock. The first effort failed, scratching the inside of her cheek. She grunted a muffled curse.

She'd have to update her Tetanus vaccination once she was back home. Refusing to give up, she went for another attempt. A few flakes of rust later and the sock snagged on the nail. Rearing her head back, the cotton and nylon blend sock was pulled from her mouth. A coughing, spitting fit followed.

"Yuck." She shuddered.

God, what she wouldn't give for a big tall glass of water about now. Better yet, her Glock and her cell phone. Fat lot of good the cell phone would do her. Service sucked out here. What she really wanted was her hands free and to find her weapon—or any weapon.

With no handy sharp objects on which to attempt cutting her bindings, she tugged harder and twisted her hands to get some slack in the ropes. The binding felt like the same cotton type rope around her ankles. Lucky for her, cotton stretched.

The moaning started again. Jess stilled. The sound came from the direction of the door on the other side of the room. Despite never having had ballet or yoga classes, she managed to hop that way while simultaneously twisting her hands.

She turned her back to the door and grabbed hold of the knob. She gave it a turn and shuffled forward, awkwardly pulling the door open. When she executed an about face the smell hit her, made her gag hard.

That moan came again, louder this time.

The possibility that one or more of those missing women could still be alive had her heart pounding even harder.

The room was dark except for the meager glow that followed Jess from the other room. She squeezed her eyes shut and then blinked rapidly to focus. The stench of decomposition was irrefutable. Someone was here and alive... but there was death down here too. Her stomach did some major protesting. She feared this would be the kind of scene no agent looked forward to discovering.

Jess hopped forward, lost her balance and hit the floor again. Her knees throbbed. She struggled upward and started moving again. She kept at the bindings around her wrists, stretching and twisting. Something dragged across her face. Felt like a spider web. She jerked back, almost fell again. She peered at what she decided was a string. The string led up to a light fixture.

Using her teeth, she got a hold on the string and pulled. Light filled the space, making her squint against the brightness.

Another moan, louder, more frantic. Other side of the room. Jess twisted in that direction. Her breath fled her lungs. She stilled as her brain assimilated what her eyes saw.

Cages... four—no, five of them.

Bare skin...arms and legs. Long dark hair... blonde hair. *Blood.*

"Oh my God."

"Help us."

The dark-haired woman raised her head. Sunken, red-rimmed eyes stared out at Jess.

Adrenaline seared through her. She jerked at her bindings, somehow squeezed her hands free, then reached down and loosened the ropes around her ankles. Fighting back the nearly overwhelming urge to heave, she rushed to the cages.

"Marie Duncan?" Jess dropped to her knees, winced, and inspected the padlock on the cage door.

The dark-haired woman nodded. "Please," she pleaded, "you have to help my sister."

Jess gave her the most reassuring smile she could muster. "That's why I'm here. To help you."

She needed a key. Dammit! She needed to call for help. Moving quickly, she checked the next two cages, careful of the body fluids that had spread across the floor. Shawna Johnston. Deceased. Her state of decomposition suggested she'd been dead several weeks.

Larissa Stone, deceased as well. Looked as if she had been dead for nearly as long as Johnston.

The fourth and fifth cages were empty.

Jess moved back to the first cage. "Marie?" She waited until the woman was looking at her. "I'm going to find the key so I can get you out of there. Okay?"

Marie shook her head. She stared down at the woman in her arms. "You have to help my sister first."

Jess's heart fell. The sister was dead. How did she get the poor woman to understand? She thought of Lily. If she and Lil were in those cages and—

A scream filled the air.

Jess whipped around. The gun registered first... then Delia Potter's face rushing toward her.

CHAPTER NINE

The second glass of wine on top of the beer she'd had at the pub was a bad idea.

Exhaustion. Dehydration. No dinner. Jess was already down three strikes before she started and still she hadn't said no. That was the problem, when it came to Dan she'd never been able to say no.

Otherwise she wouldn't be here in his urban apartment, snuggled on the worn comfortable leather sofa listening to him talk about his work.

"I kept both the mayor and the chief of police out of trouble on that one. Not an easy task, I can tell you. But I love it."

Jess laughed, knowing that was what he expected. Truth was she wasn't even assimilating the words. She was too busy watching his face, listening to his voice.

It was just plain wrong that after a whole decade he could mesmerize her as if she were seventeen again. As if they'd never fallen apart.

"I'm not saying another word," he announced, that smile teasing her.

She blinked. Had she missed something? "What?" She sipped her wine. Hoped she hadn't ignored a response cue.

"I've spent the last half hour talking about nothing but work—my work." He poured himself another glass of wine, set the nearly empty bottle back on the coffee table. "You're supposed to be telling me about you."

He grinned and her heart squeezed so tight she feared it would just stop beating altogether. "You said you'd just gotten a big promotion. I want to know what's it like to be Special Agent Jess Harris, field investigator for the F...B...I."

While she struggled to summon the ability to speak, he freshened her glass, emptying the last of the wine from the bottle. At this rate she'd need a cab to get to Lil's.

"Actually," she said finally, "I'm a profiler now."

"Hey! That's the job you always talked about." She didn't miss the glimmer of regret in his eyes before he smiled. "Congratulations." He tapped his glass to hers.

The sincerity in his voice made her happier than she would admit in a million years despite that fleeting look of regret she was sure she'd seen. Whatever else he felt, somehow his approval still meant a great deal to her. Not a good thing. "Thank you."

"Well?" he prompted, a big grin stealing her breath all over again. "Tell me more."

Surrendering to the inevitable, she kicked off her shoes and curled her feet under her to get more comfortable. She told him about BAU and her boss, Gant. The more she talked the more she had to say. It was as if they were back in college sharing future plans. The words poured out of her.

When she finally shut up he just stared at her. During that seemingly endless moment she wanted more than anything in this world for him to be proud of her.

"Jess." The pride that filled his eyes made her pulse flutter erratically. "I am genuinely happy for you." He stared at his glass for a moment and she knew he was remembering. "You knew what you wanted and you made it happen. You said you would and you did."

She'd had just enough to drink to admit that something else she'd always wanted was him... but she would take that secret to her grave. She touched her throat. *Almost had.*

"Sometimes," she confessed, "I wake up and I have to remind myself it's real." Images and voices from cases she had worked passed through her mind. None were pretty. But they represented success and accomplishment, two things that meant a great deal to her. More importantly, they meant justice for the innocent.

"You have a boyfriend?" One corner of his mouth quirked. "A husband I haven't heard about?"

She downed a big gulp of wine before she attempted to answer that one. The sweetness fizzed in her throat. Her head spun just a little. "No boy-friend. No husband." She'd noticed he wasn't wearing a wedding band. And the tour of his place hadn't revealed any indications of a female presence. "What about you? Wife? Kids?"

The idea that he might have a child pained her somehow.

Dumb, Jess.

"No wife. No kids. Not even a girlfriend." He looked away a moment. "I had a very unpleasant divorce a few months ago." He shrugged, made a disparaging sound. "The good news is I lived through it and life goes on."

Seemed an odd way to describe surviving a divorce. "It does indeed." No one knew that better than her. A subject best left alone. She cleared her throat. Time for a less sensitive topic—if not a less painful one. "How's your father and... your mother?"

He smiled. "Nice of you to ask, Agent Harris."

Jess couldn't help a chuckle. "Despite popular opinion, I would never wish your mother ill will."

"Katherine is Katherine," he said. "She stays busy with one charity event or another and that makes her happy. My father and I are both grateful."

"I'm certain she's pleased to have you helping out whenever possible."

"More importantly," he countered, "I'm pleased. When Mother isn't consumed with a project, she's lining up social activities for my father or, worse, playing matchmaker for me."

That shouldn't have bothered Jess but it did. "She wants her only son to be happy." There was no ignoring the hint of bitterness in her tone and she hated herself for letting it show. "Lil does it to me all the time," she added for cover, hoping he wouldn't notice her slip.

"That's what mothers and sisters do I guess." He set his glass on the table. "My father's doing great. He's thinking of retiring."

Dan senior was too young for retirement. Worry cleared the resentment she felt whenever Katherine Burnett came to mind. "Is he okay?"

"A mild heart attack a few months ago but he's good now. He's following the doctor's orders. I'd be willing to wager he's in better shape now than me."

Why hadn't Lil told her? Then again, she hadn't mentioned Dan's divorce either. Possibly Lil hadn't mentioned anything related to the Burnett family because Jess had told her over and over that it had been ten years. She had moved on. Lil was only honoring Jess's wishes.

Still made her mad. How ridiculous was that?

"I'm glad he's doing well." Wow. It seemed impossible they were talking about Dan's father and a heart attack. As the saying went, time marched on and everything changed. People grew older. Lil's kids hardly knew their Aunt Jess.

The surge of regret that accompanied that last thought had her wishing she hadn't let so much time pass without spending more of it with the people she cared about.

"Don't do that."

She frowned before she could stop the reaction. "Do what?" She savored more of the wine, pretending not to know what he meant. She couldn't change how much time she'd let slip by but she was here now, she told herself for the tenth time.

"Don't beat yourself up for not being around," Dan said gently. He knew her too well. "You went after your dream and you made it happen. You did it, Jess. I guess you didn't need me after all."

For about five seconds she couldn't speak, couldn't move. His words stabbed through her and the ability to respond deserted her.

"This was nice, but I do have to go." Somehow she was on her feet. She placed her glass on the table next to his, grabbed her purse and hurried across the room for her coat. Why in the world had she let this happen? This visit was about her sister and her family. Taking this unexpected detour was ridiculous and selfish. Foolish tears stung her eyes.

Oh hell. He'd done it now. Dan caught her at the door. She jerked away from his touch. "I'm sorry, Jess. That was *my* guilt talking. It was me. Not you."

All this time he'd wished they could make amends and the first chance that comes along he screws it up! Had to be the wine or just plain stupidity.

"Don't leave like this," he pleaded. The last thing he wanted was for another ten years to pass with these bad feelings standing between them.

She held up a hand in a stop gesture. The anger in her eyes shouted clearly and loudly that she wanted away from him. "It was good to see you, Dan. But I really do have to go."

Jesus Christ. He'd done it. Hurt her all over again. He was a damned fool. "I understand."

She reached for the door. "Good night."

But he couldn't let her go without trying to make this right. He put his hand over hers when she would have opened the door. "Merry Christmas, Jess. Seeing you tonight means more to me than you will ever know."

She hesitated and then looked up at him with those sweet brown eyes. His heart lurched. "Merry Christmas," she murmured.

Every part of him yearned to say more… to touch her… to taste her. Unable to resist, he leaned closer.

Her breath caught, even that soft sound made him crazy with need.

His lips touched hers and desire rushed through him. All those old feelings resurrected, made him ache for her in ways he knew would never be possible again.

Her purse and coat hit the floor and he pulled her soft body into his arms.

She would hate him for taking advantage of the moment but he was helpless to stop himself.

Jess was home and that was all that mattered.

CHAPTER TEN

ONE DAY EARLIER...
RUCKERSVILLE

Jess dove for the floor, landing on her right side. She grunted with the impact. She rolled. The discharge of the weapon exploded around her. The ping of the bullet on the concrete made her cringe.

"Don't move!" Potter screamed.

Jess froze.

With eight years in the Bureau she'd finally achieved the position at the BAU she wanted. She was a profiler now. There weren't supposed to be any more dangerous field operations.

Damn, she didn't want to die today.

"Get up!" Potter grabbed Jess's arm with her free hand.

Jess allowed the woman to drag her to her feet. Potter's forearm went around Jess's neck, the muzzle of the gun she recognized as her Glock rammed into her skull.

"Don't think I'm going to make this easy on you." Potter muttered curses as she hauled Jess toward the cages. "This is where you're going to die. That's what happens when you stick your nose in places you don't belong. All I wanted to do was get on with my life."

Jess forced sympathy into her voice. "You must've been horrified when you discovered what they'd done."

Potter made an indignant sound, then pressed her lips close to Jess's ear. "I should've put Melvin out of his misery as soon as I found that other one." She nudged Jess's temple with the muzzle. "Just look at 'em. They're pathetic. Didn't even try to fight for their lives. Whined and cried. Please don't hurt me," she mocked. "Just let us go. We'll never tell."

Jess resisted the emotions tugging at her. She had to focus. To stay alert. Survival depended on it.

Marie Duncan sobbed quietly, her sister's frail body held against her chest. The sight almost undid Jess's determination. The women were nude, their bodies covered with the signs of extreme physical abuse. All four were bone thin from malnutrition. Water and food bowls, the kind used for large dogs, sat empty in the cages. How long had it been since they'd had either? It was a miracle Marie was still alive.

Inside, Jess stilled. Marie being alive confirmed one thing. Old Melvin had at least one accomplice besides the dead guy upstairs.

"They're not strong like you," Jess offered. No need for her to guess who that other accomplice was.

"Damn straight," Potter growled. "But Melvin still wanted to play with them. It made him feel like a man to watch them plead for mercy. A real woman like me couldn't keep him happy. I didn't mean to, he'd say," she mocked. "It's the bad thoughts, he'd whine. Bastard."

Jess hoped she would be able to make sure this bitch got what was coming to her. "We can make him pay, Delia. The evidence I told you would help is right here. We can make sure Melvin gets the death sentence. After what he's put you through, we can even arrange for you to watch him die."

Potter laughed. "Right. I guess it won't matter that I left these four down here to starve after I slit Dale's sorry ass throat. You're a liar, Agent Harris. Just like all the others." She shoved Jess toward an empty cage. She landed on her knees. "Get in."

Hard as she tried, Jess couldn't keep the anger at bay. She glared up at Potter. "You should've gotten on that plane, Delia. We'd all still be thinking this was Melvin's work if you hadn't put in a personal appearance."

"You think I don't know that?" she roared. "I should've flattened all your tires. Maybe then I could've done what I needed to do and gotten out of here before you showed up." She grunted a self-deprecating sound. "I wanted to take care of this mess the last time I was here but those two Duncan bitches were still breathing. I couldn't exactly call the cops with potential witnesses against me alive in the basement. Burning the place down would've aroused suspicion. All I had to do was wait for them to die and make the call. Oh, officer," she cried, blinking her eyes rapidly as if to hold back tears, "I came to check on Dale and look what I found."

Her expression turning cruel, she glared at Jess. "Then you showed up. Now we're both screwed, Harris." She kicked Jess in the stomach. She doubled over, fighting for breath. "Get in the cage before I shoot you dead, then I'd miss the best part."

Think, Jess! Once she was in that cage, there was nothing she could do. Marie Duncan's quiet sobbing underscored that reality.

There was only one option.

She looked up at Potter. "Make me."

Fury twisted the woman's face. She leaned down, stuck the barrel of the Glock against Jess's forehead. "Get in or I'll blow your brains all over the floor."

Jess wished she hadn't let so much time pass without visiting her sister. There were things she should have said more often… things she shouldn't have taken for granted.

Then she did the only thing she could. She rolled to her side as she swung both feet and knocked Potter's out from under her.

Potter hit the floor. The weapon discharged. Flew from her hand.

Jess dove for the Glock. Potter kicked out her right foot. Barely missing a boot to the jaw, Jess scrambled after her weapon.

Potter lunged at her, threw her body atop Jess's.

Marie wailed, her cries rising with the frenzy of the struggle.

Jess focused on getting to the Glock first.

Potter grabbed her by the hair and held her back. Jess ignored the pain, stretched her arm as far as she could, her fingertips grazing the grip.

Potter reached over Jess's head. Jess elbowed her in the face. The woman howled, released Jess and clutched at her nose.

Jess snatched up the Glock just as Potter snagged her by the hair again. Ramming the muzzle into her chest, Jess warned, "Get off me!"

Potter stilled.

"Get off me," Jess repeated, her hands shaking with the effort required to refrain from pulling the trigger.

Potter released her hold on Jess's hair. She scurried away on all fours and cowered in the corner.

Getting to her feet, Jess shoved the mass of tangled hair out of her face. She hurried to the cage where Marie still rocked her sister's body. She'd stopped crying and was humming softly.

"I told Melvin I didn't want to know about his sick urges," Potter railed. "He and Dale could do whatever they wanted as long as they left me out of it." She hissed a mouthful of curses. "He shouldn't have ignored my rules. Keeping one at his house was the last straw. I fixed him."

Jess didn't have time to listen to her sick ramblings. She needed to help Marie. Get her out of that damned cage. What she really needed was a phone.

"Get in the cage." Jess pointed to the one Potter had tried to force her into.

Potter didn't move. "I didn't do anything wrong. I'm only guilty of looking the other way."

"I guess Pritchard cut his own throat."

"He was still feeding them," Potter ranted. "He had no right doing that. Melvin was the boss. He wasn't supposed to do anything without Melvin's say so. I told him to let them die and then we'd bury them."

Wasn't she just the epitome of compassion? "Stay on your hands and knees and get in there. *Now.*"

Potter crawled toward the cage. Jess gave her a wide berth until she was inside and then she latched the door and snapped the padlock in place. "Is there a landline in the house?"

Potter smiled up at Jess. "I cut the line. Threw the phone in the trash. Don't worry about it, Agent Harris. None of us are getting out of here. We're all going to die."

Jess ignored her but there was no denying the bad, bad feeling that suddenly stirred in the pit of her stomach. "We'll see about that."

She needed keys or bolt cutters to get into the other cages.

"Don't waste your time," Potter said. "They're all dead but one and she's on her way out."

"Where's the key to those locks?" She was amazed by how much she wanted to shoot Delia Potter. Save the Commonwealth a pile of money.

"Threw 'em away."

Damn. "What about bolt cutters?" Jess scrutinized the shelves.

"There's a pair hanging over there." Potter gestured across the room. "Have at it. Take all the time you need."

Jess grabbed the bolt cutters and snapped the locks on the cages. She tossed the tool aside and knelt at the door of the cage that held the Duncan sisters. Putting the two in one cage to die together had likely been part of the torture.

"Marie, let me help you climb out," Jess urged. The smell of feces and urine was overpowering. Bonita had been dead maybe a day. Rigor had already started to reverse.

Marie shook her head. "Help my sister first."

Jess opened her mouth to explain but Marie interrupted. "She's my baby sister. It's my job to protect her..." Her voice broke. "Please, help her."

Marie was weak. Her face, particularly around her eyes, was sunken. Her body had that emaciated look. She needed medical attention right now. Holding onto her sister's body posed even more risks. Her best chance of survival was if Jess drove her to town. She could call for help as soon as she had cell service but there was no time to wait.

None of that mattered to Marie Duncan. Her only concern was for her sister. Jess scrubbed at her aching forehead. She needed Marie's cooperation. "Okay, we'll get Bonita out first."

Potter laughed.

Jess glared at her.

"You're wasting precious time, Harris," Potter taunted.

Then Jess smelled it… *smoke.*

She rushed to the stairs, taking them two at a time, Potter's laughter following her. The stairs led into the kitchen. The room was full of smoke. Flames were eating away at the wall between the kitchen and whatever was on the other side. The living room, she thought.

"Dammit!" Jess ran to the back door and wrenched it open.

The sky was dark but the full moon illuminated the snow.

"Shit!" She hurried back down the stairs. There was no time. She had to get Marie out of this basement.

Potter laughed even louder. Jess ignored her. She shoved the Glock into the waistband of her slacks and reached into the cage for Marie.

She drew away. "Help my sister first."

Jess searched the woman's eyes, needed her to see the truth in her words as she spoke. "Marie, your sister is dead. You have to come with me now. The house is on fire and we have to get out of here."

Marie shook her head. "I won't leave her."

"Listen to me, Marie," Jess said more firmly, "I'm with the FBI. You have to do as I say now."

"If you had a sister you'd understand," Marie said, her voice growing weaker. "I can't leave her. I *won't* leave her."

"Goodbye, Agent Harris!" Potter taunted. "We're all going to die."

CHAPTER ELEVEN

Dan swept her into his arms. Jess curled hers around his neck, her fingers threaded into his hair. How many times had she dreamed of touching him this way? The way she had a thousand times before. Her mind had relived over and over, even when she didn't want to, the memories permanently etched across her heart and soul.

He carried her away from the door. She drew back from his kiss to get her bearings. They moved into his bedroom. Fear or maybe good sense shook her. What was she doing?

He must have felt her tension because before she could protest, he settled her on the foot of his bed and dropped to his knees. "I've missed you so much, Jess."

His hands cupped her face and he tenderly kissed her cheeks, her chin, and down the column of her throat. His beard rasped against her skin, sending shivers cascading over her. Heat stirred, chasing away the cold that nothing else had been able to touch in the last twenty-four hours.

His fingers trailed down her arms, his warm lips stilled at the base of her throat. He reached up, caressed her bruised skin softly. "Who hurt you?"

She didn't want to talk about that. In that pivotal moment she understood that what she wanted was to forget about those hours in that basement... to forget about all the years that stood between her and this man. She wanted to feel those wonderful sensations only Dan could ignite in her. She wanted him. Now. No talking.

She grasped the hem of her sweater and pulled it up and off while he watched, worry still lining his beautiful face. She tossed the garment aside. "No more talking."

He tugged at the buttons of his shirt, kissing her even as his fingers fumbled with one closure after the other. She reached behind her, unfastened her bra and let it fall away. He made a sound in his throat that emboldened her further. She no longer cared what day it was or how much time had passed since they had been together like this.

His fingers splayed across her torso, caressed her as his mouth tortured her breasts. She surrendered to the pleasure. Every tug of his lips had the ache between her thighs growing more and more unbearable.

He dragged off her shoes, helped her to her feet, then unfastened her slacks. As the fabric slid down her legs, he sat back on his heels and watched, the amazement in his expression tearing at her heart.

Her legs trembling, she settled back on the bed. He kissed her bruised knees. Kissed his way up her thighs. When he reached her belly button he urged her down onto the cool sheets. He stilled. She knew he was considering the bruises there too. His lips soothed the sore muscles of her abdomen as he dragged her silky panties down her skin. The muscles deep inside her started that rhythmic pulsing. His mouth moved to that part of her and she couldn't hold back any longer. Her fingers fisted in the sheets as she cried out with pleasure.

He did nearly unbearable things to her with nothing more than his lips and tongue until she begged him to stop. He just smiled and started a slow, delicious path up her torso, tasting, sucking, and touching every part of her he encountered. Soothing the bruises with extra attention.

Somehow her fingers found the closure of his trousers, she got them loosened and shoved them along with his boxers down his hips. He was more than ready, erect and hard, smooth and hot. She wrapped her legs around his waist and forced that part of him toward the ache that was making her writhe in delicious agony.

He lifted her bottom until the tip of him was just barely inside her.

She gasped. Couldn't move... couldn't speak... she could only feel.

He pushed in another inch. They both made a sound that came from the fiercest of primal need— the kind of need that defied articulation.

Slowly, an inch at a time, as if he wanted to savor every part of the act, he filled her. Opened her fully, the way only he ever had. Then he put his face close enough to nuzzle hers. The feel of his lips, the heat of his breath whispered across her cheek as he gave her a moment to adjust to all of him. Then he started to rock his hips so incredibly gently.

He cradled her face in his hands and stared deep into her eyes. "I want to show you how many ways I've missed you." He took her mouth with his own and kissed her as if it might be the last time he ever kissed anyone.

His gentle rocking grew harder, faster and she lost herself completely. She screamed with an orgasm unlike any she'd experienced since the last time they'd made love. Her legs still wrapped around his waist, he held her tight against his chest as he stood, their bodies remaining intimately connected. She laid her head against his shoulder while he kicked free of the trousers and boxers puddled around his ankles.

He carried her to the window, sat her naked bottom on the cool, marble ledge. He pulled back, almost all the way, then slid into her, and repeated the motions over and over. The rhythm was slow, the thrusts deep. His skin was so hot. Every place he touched her he set a fire even as the cold glass at her back and the chilly marble beneath her bottom tried to cool her. He nibbled at her ear… teased her chin with his teeth, never losing that perfect tempo.

He suddenly slowed, peered out the window beyond her. "Every time," he said breathlessly, "I look at those lights I think of you. It's the reason I chose this place."

She tightened her legs around his waist, took him in as deep as her body would allow. "Come here." She pulled his face down to hers and kissed him solidly on the mouth. He lifted her against him and carried her back to the bed. He laid her there and came down on top of her without breaking that kiss or the perfect bond of their bodies. Mere seconds later she was ready to come again.

He made love to her over and over. Fast and hard. Slow and tender. She came more times than she could remember. Over and over he kissed every part of her that was bruised and damaged by the evil she had survived.

The last time he came he collapsed beside her, pulled her to him and whispered something unintelligible in her ear.

The words followed her to sleep and somewhere along the way she was certain he repeated them.

I will always love you.

CHAPTER TWELVE

RUCKERSVILLE

"Shut up!" Jess demanded. She had to think.

She wasn't sure Marie could walk out of here. Maybe Potter could carry Bonita and Jess could carry Marie.

The flames whooshed, the sound roaring down the stairs. The house grumbled.

"Hear that," Potter said. "It'll all come down any second now."

Jess grabbed the bolt cutters and snapped the lock on Potter's cage. "Let's go," she ordered. Crazy bitch or not, she couldn't leave her here to die. No matter how much she wanted to. "You can help me."

Potter shook her head. "I think I'll just stay." She crossed her arms over her chest.

"If you help me," Jess said, trying another tactic, "your actions could help your case. Could make things easier on you."

"I'm not spending the rest of my life in prison. I'd rather stay put and hear you scream when the flames devour you."

To hell with her. "You can come or not. Makes no difference to me."

Jess knelt at the door to the sisters' cage once more. "Marie, we have to go now. I need you to let go of your sister and climb out."

"Please." She shook her head. "I can't leave her. She's all I have in the world."

Jess battled back the emotions ramming at her. "Maybe we can do this together."

Marie helped Jess get her sister through the small opening, then she crawled out. She tried to stand. Couldn't. Her legs were too weak.

Jess started to place Bonita's body on the floor.

"No!" Marie shook her head. "Carry her. I'll crawl."

They made it as far as the stairs, Potter's taunts playing like a bad musical score to low-budget horror flick.

Marie couldn't manage the stairs. Jess squatted next to her. "Put your arms around my neck and hang on."

As the frail woman wrapped her arms around her, Jess did something she hadn't done in a very long time. She prayed. She prayed for the strength to make it up the stairs with Marie hanging onto her back and a dead woman in her arms.

The first step was the most difficult. The rest were a blur.

When they reached the kitchen the smoke was so thick Jess could hardly breathe. Her throat and eyes burned. How the hell was she going to do this?

The room was engulfed in flames. Holding Bonita close to her chest, she dropped to the floor.

"Marie, I want you to crawl now. Stay right behind me. Don't let go of my coat."

Throat and lungs burning, they made it to the backdoor. Thank God she'd left it open otherwise she might never have found it, confusion was already wreaking havoc with her judgment.

No sooner than she was knee deep in snow, something inside the house collapsed.

With Marie hanging onto her neck once more, Jess trudged through the snow until they were almost to her car. Exhausted, she dropped to her knees. Couldn't carry both women any farther. She coughed until she lost her breath.

When she could breathe again, she stared up at the moon. Every part of her was drained and aching. The sound of the flames and the crackling of the wood resonated in the night.

"See I told you," Marie whispered as she reached out to her sister, "we're free and we're going home."

Somehow Jess got up. Her eyes were stinging. Had to be the smoke. Rather than argue with Marie again, she carried Bonita to her car first. Then she helped Marie into the back seat next to her. Thankfully her keys were still in the ignition. Jess opened the trunk and got her blanket to cover the two women.

She collapsed behind the wheel and started the engine. Her feet were numb. Behind her, Marie was singing softly to her sister. Jess understood she was operating on adrenaline. She hoped it held out until she could get her to a hospital. Marie was in far worse condition than she realized.

The digital clock on the radio showed ten minutes before midnight. *Almost Christmas Eve.*

Eyes and throat burning like hell, Jess turned her car around and drove away. In her rearview mirror she saw the sparks fly as the house started to collapse in onto itself. They'd barely made it. She had no idea if Potter had run out or if she'd died in that basement. Something for local law enforcement to figure out.

At the main road, two SUVs skidded to a stop in front of Jess's car.

Even in the moonlight she recognized Gant and Taylor as they emerged from one of the vehicles and rushed toward her. Jess put her car into park and collapsed against the seat. Thank God.

Gant jerked her door open. "What the hell happened? You okay?"

"Marie and Bonita Duncan are in the backseat," Jess reported. "Marie's alive. The others are dead." She closed her eyes against the images.

She could hear Taylor calling for backup. Someone was in the backseat checking on Marie. Like the devoted sister she was, Marie insisted Bonita needed attention first.

"You hurt, Harris?" Gant demanded.

Jess nodded. "I'm okay."

"We've got one deceased and one alive. She needs a hospital now," a male voice said from the backseat.

Before Jess could tell him Marie had a name, another man she didn't recognize was suddenly helping to lift Marie from the backseat. The woman cried for them to take her sister first. They ignored her.

"Tell them to take the sister too." Jess closed her eyes and fought the tears as images of Lily played through her thoughts. Life was too short. No one had the promise of tomorrow. Not going home for so long was wrong.

"The sister's dead," Gant said as if she didn't know that already.

"Please." Jess opened her eyes, swiped at the tears. "Marie needs her sister with her."

Gant pulled back from the door and shouted the order to the men loading Marie into one of the SUVs. Whatever they thought about his order, they obeyed.

With the Duncan sisters secured inside, the SUV tore out into the night, headed for the nearest hospital.

Jess said another swift prayer for Marie. Funny how she was suddenly doing all this praying.

"Come on, Harris," Gant said, tugging at her arm. "I'm taking you to the hospital just to be sure." He glanced at the SUV roaring away, then at the old farmhouse now totally engulfed in flames. "Jesus Christ. I think it's time you took that vacation you keep putting off."

Jess stared up at him. For about three seconds she couldn't speak. The emotions expanded so fast inside her she thought she might die right there in her almost new car with her new boss staring at her. "I don't need medical attention. I just want to go home."

To Birmingham.

CHAPTER THIRTEEN

CHRISTMAS DAY
BIRMINGHAM, 6:15 A.M.

Jess opened her eyes. Her heart beat faster as Dan's face came into focus. She'd been dreaming about the farmhouse... and the fire. Remembered fear quaked through her.

Dan was still asleep. She should go before he woke. She realized this but her body refused to obey. She wanted to look at him for just a minute more. She knew every single detail... but there were small changes since the last time she'd seen him. A line or two here or there. Mostly he was just as handsome as before, maybe more so.

Memories flooded her and tears brimmed on her lashes. They had been inseparable in high school and in college. Had made so many plans. They'd had their whole lives mapped out.

But those dreams had died as surely as those women had died in that farmhouse. No one had come to rescue them in time.

Marie Duncan had survived. Gant had called Jess on the way here to let her know Marie would recover. Marie hadn't cared whether she survived or not, only that her sister got the help she needed. *If you had a sister you would understand... I can't leave her... I won't leave her.*

When had Jess forgotten how important family was? When had work become her only priority? She'd sacrificed too much.

Even him.

She resisted the urge to reach out and touch Dan. Just looking at him made her yearn for things that would never be.

More memories washed over her. The shouting. Him telling her he was leaving. Her daring him to go. *If you don't love me any more than that, just go!*

She'd come home from work the next day and he was gone. Part of her had refused to believe he would stay away... but she'd been wrong.

For months after that she had argued with herself about who did what and who was right. The truth was she and Dan had fallen apart while they weren't looking. Both of them had been so busy with school and work, there just hadn't been time to notice the slow, steady disintegration. Their future plans had continued as if simply saying they were moving ahead with the wedding would somehow hold them together.

Pretending hadn't been enough.

He had left her. Anguish twisted her heart. Dan had left her all alone to the life they had planned together for years.

What in the world was she doing here?

There was no going back for either of them. She couldn't undo the past any more than he could.

She had achieved the position she'd hoped for... the one she'd spent her entire career to date striving toward. That was her life now. His life was here. He wouldn't want to change his life anymore than she would.

But there were some mistakes she could make sure she never repeated. She was never going to take her sister for granted again. Not for a second.

Moving carefully so as not to wake him, she eased out of the bed. She gathered her scattered clothes and hastily dressed. The bruises on her knees and abdomen, not to mention her throat, were an even uglier shade of blue and green today. Her wrists were scraped and burned from struggling with the ropes. She glanced in the mirror and winced. She looked a fright. But she was alive. Maybe more so than she had been in a long time.

At the bedroom door she paused. She shouldn't look back. It wasn't smart. Still she looked. The white pillowcase looked stark beneath his dark hair. She closed her eyes and savored the smell of him one last time... and the lingering scent of their lovemaking.

Time to go.

She turned away.

Lily and her family were waiting.

It was Christmas.

The sound of the door closing woke Dan. He sat up, stared at the empty place on the bed next to him.

She was gone.

His heart sank and all the hope he'd dared to feel died, taking a piece of him with it. He picked up the pillow she'd slept on and hugged it to his chest, closed his eyes and inhaled her sweet scent.

He wished he had known the right words to make her stay. He'd been wrong to leave the way he had all those years ago. The truth was he'd been terrified. No matter how hard he tried he never measured up to her. Not that she kept score, but he did.

His ego had caused him to make the biggest mistake of his life.

But she had kept moving forward without him. She'd achieved her dreams. Something he hadn't been able to do, not entirely anyway. Two failed marriages attested to that sad fact.

Ultimately that was the trouble between him and Jess. He opened his eyes and exhaled a big breath. There was no keeping her here. From the moment he'd laid eyes on her she'd informed him that she had a plan.

No force on earth was going to stop her from following her dream and making it a reality.

Nothing wrong with that… except it didn't include him.

Or maybe he just hadn't been able to keep up.

Lakefront Trail, Bessemer, 8:15 a.m.

As promised, Lil had left the front door unlocked for Jess. She slipped in, gifts for the kids under each arm. Lil, Blake, and their children were in the family room gathered around the Christmas tree. Torn wrapping paper and bows were scattered all over the floor.

Jess grinned. "Merry Christmas!"

Lil looked up. The happiness that beamed from her face squeezed Jess's heart.

"Jess!" Lil jumped up and rushed to hug her. "You're here! I can't believe it!"

Alice and Blake junior ran over to get their gifts and to welcome their Aunt Jess. Blake senior got a hug in too.

Jess tried her best not to cry but after what happened in Ruckersville and then last night with Dan it was difficult. She joined the family around the tree. Watching made her breath catch. They were so happy. Lil was such a good mother.

Some errant brain cell had Jess wondering if she had come back with Dan ten years ago, would they have all this by now? The house, the kids?

No looking back.

"Hey!" Blake junior shouted. "It's snowing!"

They all hurried to the window and watched the falling snow. The white stuff was no novelty in Virginia, but here it was a special treat.

It was good to be with family for Christmas.

Jess wondered if Dan was watching the falling snow too. For just one second she wished he were here.

Only because it was Christmas.

Read on for a special sneak peek at <u>VICIOUS</u>,
book 7 of the Faces of Evil series!

VICIOUS

FACES OF EVIL

DEBRA WEBB

"The age of our fathers, which was
worse than that of our ancestors,
produced us, who are about to raise a progeny
more vicious than ourselves."
~Horace

CHAPTER ONE

TWELVE HOURS EARLIER...

"Do you know who I am?"

His guest moved her head side to side in swift, frantic little shakes. Her dark eyes were round with fear and every desperate breath echoed that same fear in the quiet room.

Satisfaction made him smile. She was unaware of his name or his reputation, yet she instinctively understood that her life as she knew it was at an end.

Rory Stinnett was going to die.

How fortunate she was to be the first chosen to join him in this final round of the game that would ensure his place in the annals of modern history. Before the last ounce of life drained from her, she would know the name Eric Spears intimately. And he would know every sweet, luscious part of her, inside and out.

This one was truly beautiful. Long, silky hair as black as the deepest part of the night. He traced the length of her throat with his eyes. She shivered as if he'd stroked his fingers there. Her extraordinarily sculpted body lay naked before him. The restraints at her wrists, waist and ankles, chaffed her smooth, tanned skin.

His gaze lingered on her breasts, nipples erect from the low temperature in the room or from the terror coursing through her veins, either way they begged for attention. Anticipation stirred inside him. Not yet, it wasn't time to play. Her role in the game was immensely important, far more so than she could possibly comprehend.

"You will know me in time." His promise prompted another delicious shiver of her exquisite body.

"But not until the perfect moment," he explained. "Not until the others are here."

Not until *she* was here.

His body tightened with excitement as the image of the guest of honor for the upcoming coup de grace filled his mind.

Once Jess was here, the final game would begin.

He could hardly wait.

CHAPTER TWO

Deputy Chief Jess Harris waited in the cramped private room for the patient to decide she was ready to continue. The uncomfortable plastic chair squeaked each time Jess shifted. She crossed her legs to stop her knee from bouncing with impatience and frustration. Didn't help. Her worst nightmare was coming true and she couldn't just sit here and pretend she wasn't worried.

Eric Spears, the sociopathic serial killer who haunted her every waking hour, had taken his first victim. Equal measures of fury and fear erupted inside her all over again. She struggled to hold back the emotions welling up in her throat. Breaking down at this point wouldn't help anyone, least of all the woman he'd chosen to use in his sadistic plan.

As soon as Jess received word from the Bureau that two of the three missing women had been found,

103

she and Chief of Police Dan Burnett were on their way. With no nonstop flights out of Birmingham, Alabama, they'd had to endure a plane change in Atlanta. Every wasted minute had cranked Jess's tension a little higher. By the time they arrived in Knoxville, the Bureau and local law enforcement had already finished their interviews and she was ready to snap.

Unless the two survivors of this perverted reality game could provide some additional insight into where Spears had held them or why he hadn't freed the third victim or what he intended next, they had nothing. *Nothing at all.* Spears had made his choice from the three women abducted from Alabama ten days ago and he'd vanished with her. Not one shred of evidence had been left behind. None they had discovered at any rate.

Nausea roiled in Jess's belly. She had to find a way to stop him.

Since Claudia Brown had given Jess nothing more, her only remaining hope was to glean additional details from Melaney Lands, the woman lying in the hospital bed a few feet away. Jess shifted again in the uncomfortable chair.

Melaney, born and raised in Mobile and a nursing student at the University of South Alabama, adjusted her bendable straw with a shaky hand. She took a long draw of water from the plastic cup.

Enough time passed to have Jess's already strained nerves frayed completely. Melaney placed the cup on the tray table extended across her lap.

She clasped her hands on the white sheet tucked against the faded blue hospital gown she wore, but still she didn't speak. Jess wondered if the woman understood how very lucky she was to have survived a close encounter with Spears, the Player, a vicious serial killer who loved torturing his victims before ending their lives.

Of the thirty some odd cases of abducted women attributed to him by the Federal Bureau of Investigation, there had never been a survivor. Not one. Detective Lori Wells of Birmingham PD had met the monster and lived to tell but then he hadn't abducted her. One of his reckless minions, Matthew Reed, had taken her. That was the last mistake Reed would ever make.

It seemed impossible that nightmare had been scarcely more than a month ago.

The air stalled in Jess's lungs as her heart flailed like a fish swept onto the bank and then deserted by the tide. Everything about her life had changed. Gotten far more complicated.

God Almighty, what was she going to do?

She adjusted her glasses. Right now, she couldn't think about the other troubles stewing in her private life. There just wasn't time to linger and she couldn't afford the distraction.

"The man was smoking outside the Wash-n-Go where I do my laundry."

Startled by the sound of the woman's voice, despite having been on the edge of her seat in anticipation, Jess snapped to attention.

Melaney drew in a shuddering breath. "He was white, tall, kinda young—maybe twenty-five." She shrugged and then winced. The final twenty-four hours of captivity her hands and feet had been tied behind her back with one end of the rope around her neck. She was sore as hell with plenty of bruises and abrasions.

"He had on jeans and a tee-shirt," Melaney continued. "There was a logo but it was faded. I didn't look at him long enough to make it out."

Jess jotted a couple of notes on her pad. "According to the statements you gave earlier, this man didn't say anything to you as you exited the Laundromat."

Melaney shook her head. "He didn't. When I glanced at him he did one of those nods. You know, the one people do instead of saying hello or what's up."

"Did you nod back?" She hadn't mentioned a response, not even a gesture, but she was feeling safer now. As she relaxed more details could surface.

Another negligible shrug prompted a second wince of pain. "If I did, I don't remember doing it. I think I just looked away."

For several more seconds she didn't speak. She was remembering. The horror of that night danced across her face as easy to read as the breaking news scroll on a cable channel.

"I put my laundry bag in the back seat and closed the door, that's when I noticed the tire was flat." She clamped her lips together and still they trembled.

"You drive a 1971 Toyota Corolla?" Jess knew the answer but she needed to nudge Melaney past the shame she'd snagged on. For the rest of her life, she would question her every move from that night. Had she done this or that things might have turned out differently.

What Melaney Lands didn't grasp was that she had been chosen. Her hair color was the one he preferred. She was smart and attractive and had the right figure. She fit the profile of the women the Player selected. Nothing she did or didn't do would have made a difference.

"I've had that Corolla since I got my driver's license."

"The flat tire was on the...?" Jess held her pencil poised to take down the answer. It was the mundane that most often prodded forth the notable.

"The passenger side. Rear tire. I said shit or something like that. When I looked up he was standing right beside me. I jumped, and he apologized for scaring me. He offered to help. There wasn't anybody else around so I said okay." Tears slipped down her cheeks. "I did what anybody else would have done... I didn't—"

"If you had said no," Jess stopped her, "he would have taken a different approach, but the end result would've been the same." She held Melaney's gaze a moment more before moving on. "He fixed your tire and then what happened?"

"Damned thing wouldn't start." She knotted her fingers in the sheet, her eyes getting brighter with the fresh tears brimming there. "It was running fine... before. I guess I must've been so upset I didn't lock the doors when I got in the car. Another stupid mistake. Then suddenly he was in the passenger seat." Her lips trembled. "He used a hypodermic needle to inject a drug into my shoulder." She drew her right shoulder into her body. "When I woke up I was in a cage. There were two others... we were all in cages."

The ketamine, Spears' drug of choice, worked fast. There would have been little time or strength for a struggle. The story from both women was basically the same except for the setting. Claudia Brown, a graduate student at A&M College, lived in Somerville. She was taken by a different male suspect from the alley behind her apartment. Her cat hadn't come in for dinner. At bedtime, Claudia had gone outside to look for the missing pet that, as it turned out, was alive and well ten blocks away.

The woman Spears had kept, Rory Stinnett, was from Orange Beach. She was a student at the same university as Melaney but the two hadn't known each other until they ended up in those cages in a white room with fluorescent lights. They had described the cages as being made of heavy gauge metal wire similar to the ones used to crate large dogs. The cages allowed the women to see one another and to communicate.

Some memory Jess couldn't quite grasp nudged her. Something to do with cages.

"Once you were in the cage, you never saw anyone other than the masked man?" Jess asked. According to their statements, a man wearing a ski mask had checked on them daily. This man, they both insisted, was not the same one who had abducted either of them.

Melaney shook her head, corroborating the answer Claudia had given. After viewing catalogs of mug shots, including photos of Spears, both women had confirmed what everyone else suspected: Spears was not one of the abductors and he wasn't the masked man. There was a strong possibility that he hadn't been anywhere near these women.

His presence was irrelevant, in Jess's opinion. This was his doing whether he was at the scene of the crime or not.

He had started a new game and Jess was way behind the curve.

She blinked away the distraction. *Stay on the facts. You already know his motive.*

The women were dehydrated, bruised and emotionally wounded but that was the extent of their injuries. During those long days of captivity the man wearing a mask had dropped a bottle of water and a container of nuts and dried fruits into their cages daily. Not once had he attempted to touch the women or even to speak to them. But then torturing or murdering anyone at this stage in the game wasn't the goal—wasn't even on the agenda.

Spears had other plans.

DEBRA WEBB

"Since he didn't speak," Jess ventured, "how can you be certain the person wearing the mask was a man?" There were numerous reasons to make the assumption but she wanted to hear each woman's rationale for coming to that conclusion. The smallest new detail might make a difference.

"His hands." Melaney's brow furrowed as if she were concentrating hard on the question. "He had big hands, thick fingers."

"He didn't wear gloves?"

Another shake of her head. Just went to show the level of confidence the man had in the hiding place used for holding the women. Claudia had mentioned his broad shoulders and muscled arms as well as his hands. She'd also said he had dark eyes. Jess suspected Melaney had kept her gaze lowered whenever their keeper entered the room. Claudia, on the other hand, had studied his height, six feet at least, and his build—a little on the stocky side.

According to the descriptions provided by Melaney and Claudia, different men abducted them at approximately the same time on the same night. Both insisted Rory had described yet a third man. The event had obviously been a carefully choreographed series of steps in various locations for achieving the singular goal of a madman. The organized operation confirmed the Bureau's theory that Spears had built a network of murderous followers ready to do his bidding.

Jess dismissed the detail. She couldn't think about that and do what needed to be done here. "What happened when the two of you were finally moved from the cages?"

"He drugged us again." Melaney looked around the room as if searching for a safe place to rest her gaze. "When we came to, we were on the side of the road. Naked and all tied up."

She fell silent for a time. No doubt reliving the horrors and the relief.

"We started yelling for help. We kept screaming and crying, hoping someone would hear us. I don't know how much later—hours I guess—a trucker stopped. The guy was headed into the woods to pee when we managed to get his attention." She exhaled a shuddering breath. "We'd screamed so much by then it was a miracle he heard us."

Jess had interviewed the truck driver who discovered the women on that Tennessee mountain road. Otis Berry was short, bone thin, and sixty-eight years old. He had a bum knee that caused him to hobble and a bad back that kept him stooped over, making him easy to rule out as a suspect.

"Can you tell me anything else about Rory?" Rory Stinnett was the third woman, the one Spears had chosen to keep. *Victim number one.* Jess worked at calming another bout of churning in her stomach.

Something awful was coming. Spears had some twisted finale planned. She could feel it. And, damn it, she couldn't seem to do anything to stop it.

"We cried and talked a lot. Tried to figure out ways to escape but none of them worked." Melaney scrubbed at her tears with the backs of her hands. "We didn't know whether he was going to kill us or what. He never told us anything. Until Claudia and I were with the police we had no idea what was going on."

"I'm sure you'd seen the headlines about Eric Spears, the serial killer called the Player, before your abduction?" Just saying his name out loud changed the rhythm of Jess's heart. She tightened her grip on her pencil.

"I'm a nursing student. I don't have time for the news or anything else. But Claudia had heard of him and all those women he killed." Her voice trembled on the last.

Not just women. Jess didn't bother correcting her. Eric Spears had murdered a federal agent who'd graduated from the Bureau's training academy with her. The truth was there were likely far more victims than they suspected. They might never know just how many lives Eric Spears had taken… or would take before he was captured. Or killed.

Just let me close one more time.

"A few more questions, Miss Lands." Jess tucked her pad and pencil into her bag. "Do you remember how the place where you were held smelled? If there were any windows? Any other furniture? Could you hear any noises from the outside?"

Melaney just kept shaking her head no.

Feeling a little defeated, Jess carried on. "Do you recall anything different or strange that happened in school or at home in the week or so before you were abducted?"

The young woman stared at Jess as if she were completely overwhelmed and totally lost. Finally, she shook her head again, more tears shining in her eyes as renewed defeat clouded her face.

Jess stood and moved to the side of her bed. She placed a business card on the tray table. She wasn't usually the touchy-feely type but she gave Melaney's hand a gentle squeeze just the same. "Anything you remember or need, no matter when it is, day or night, tomorrow or weeks from now, you call me. Don't hesitate."

A jerky nod was her answer.

"Thank you, Melaney."

Jess turned and started for the door. She was thankful these two women were safe and unharmed for the most part. As grateful as she was, she wished something—anything—one or the other remembered could help them find Rory Stinnett.

How much time did they have before Stinnett became a statistic in the massive case file on the Player?

"Wait." Melaney's tinny voice resonated against the sterile white walls of her room.

Jess stopped, turned and waited. Adrenaline pumped through her. There was something different in the other woman's tone now... a new kind of fear or desperation crammed into that one word.

Melaney visibly struggled with what she had to say, as if she feared the words would somehow change what happened next. "I wasn't going to mention it." She made an aching sound. "The drug was sucking me into the darkness, and I wasn't sure if I really heard what I thought I heard. Claudia said she didn't remember anyone saying anything. I figured maybe I imagined it."

Jess's thoughts, the very blood flowing through her veins, hushed.

Melaney moistened her chapped lips. "But, when you came in here and introduced yourself, I knew I hadn't imagined it."

A chill crept into Jess's bones. "You may have seen me or heard my name on the news." Her own voice sounded strained. Her chest seemed to be rising and falling too rapidly, yet she couldn't get enough air into her lungs.

Melaney shook her head. "Told you I don't watch the news."

Jess moved closer to the foot of her bed. "All right. What do you think you heard?"

"He whispered…" Melaney struggled with whatever it was she needed to say. "Or maybe it was the drug that made his voice seem so low and quiet."

Holding her breath, Jess waited for the rest.

"He said, *tell Jess this is all for her.*"

Somehow, Jess managed a nod. "Thank you, Melaney."

When she would have turned away, Melaney's voice stopped her again. "Are *you* the reason he did this to us?"

Jess would've given just about anything to be able to say no…

Want to start the Faces of Evil from the beginning? Read the blockbuster debut of the Faces of Evil. Get OBSESSION now!

CPSIA information can be obtained at www.ICGtesting.com
Printed in the USA
LVOW10s1218051014

407330LV00001B/41/P